Last Man Standing

Alan Gibbons is a full-time writer and a visiting speaker and lecturer at schools, colleges and literary events nationwide, including the major book festivals: Edinburgh, Northern Children's Book Festival, Swansea, Cheltenham, Sheffield and Salford. Alan has recently embarked on a high profile, nationwide campaign to champion libraries and librarianship and to reevaluate government commitment to educational spending.

Last Man Standing

Alan Gibbons

Orion
Children's Books

First published in Great Britain in 1998
by Orion Children's Books
Reissued in Great Britain in 2010
by Orion Children's Books
a division of the Orion Publishing Group Ltd
Orion House
5 Upper St Martin's Lane
London WC2H 9EA
An Hachette UK company

978-1-4440-0180-8

A catalogue record for this book is available from the British Library.

www.orionbooks.co.uk

Rough Diamonds

THE SQUAD

Darren 'Daz' Kemble (goalkeeper)
Joey Bannen (defence and substitute goalkeeper)
Mattie Hughes (defence)
Anthony 'Ant' Glover (defence)
Jimmy Mintoe (defence)
Carl Bain (defence)
John O'Hara (mid-field)
Jamie Moore (mid-field)
Kevin 'Guv' McGovern (mid-field)
Bashir Gulaid (mid-field)
Pete 'Ratso' Ratcliffe (mid-field)
Dave Lafferty (striker)
Gordon Jones (striker and captain)

Manager: Bobby Jones

PART ONE

Promises Made

One

The moment you try to stand still you start to go backwards.

I came up with that gem on a hot July night as I lay in bed listening to the drunks rolling home after a night down the Liver Bird. I had a good reason for lying awake. I'd had a great night myself at the Dockers' Club. Not boozing or anything, you understand, not like the sad plonkies you get down the Birdy. I'm only eleven, for crying out loud! My mum wouldn't even let me have a sip of her wine at Gran's birthday party. No, it was business. The Dockers is where the South Sefton Junior League holds its presentations. We're the Challenge Cup winners so we were there by right. Not exactly the European Cup, you might think, but not bad when you consider where we were in mid-Autumn.

I'm Kev McGovern, by the way, the Guv'nor to my friends, a nightmare to my enemies. When I joined the Diamonds back in October last year they were propping up the table. The licking boys of the whole league, that was us. Rubbish manager, rubbish strip, rubbish name and rubbish morale. Total football? Forget it. We were total rubbish. Anybody else would have given us up as a bad job. Not me. I'm a fighter. I've had to be. My dad cleared out four years ago and when he showed up again just before Christmas he wasn't exactly riding a white charger. In fact, he was driving the BMW belonging to a slimy ratbag by the name of Lee Ramage, our friendly neighbourhood villain. That's friendly as your average scorpion understands the term. The drug dealer's little helper, that's my old feller's occupation in life. You know what he says: I deal the stuff, but I don't do it. I'm not daft. If you could make money out of daisy chains I'd be into that, too. I suppose he thinks that makes it better! Thanks, Dad, you give a kid a lot to be proud of.

Anyway, like I said, I don't take anything lying down. If I was meant to just lie there and take the grief, God would have given me a doormat for a face.

At the end of a tough season eight months later, I reckon we've got a lot to be proud of. Not only have we won the Challenge Cup, we've also clawed our way to mid-table respectability. One of our players, Dave Lafferty, has even been signed up for Everton's School of Excellence. Which brings me back to what I was saying earlier. You can't rest on your laurels. It's something our manager Ronnie Mintoe has started saying. Look at the most successful English sides since the war, he tells us. You know what Liverpool and Man United did the moment they tasted success? They had a clear-out. Brought in new blood, because the moment you lift a trophy your achievement is history. If you can't put it behind you and go forward, you're history, too. He's got a head on his shoulders, our Ronnie. Suddenly every one of us is looking over our shoulder wondering who he has in mind to take our place. We're all desperate to prove we can do it. I don't care what it takes. I don't want the Diamonds to be a flash in the pan. I want us to be living legends, and if that means changing things round then I'm with Ronnie.

There isn't much choice over Dave, of course. It's great him signing forms with Everton and all that. He could even play in the Premiership one day, but it takes him right out of Sunday League football. That's right, we're a victim of our own success. No sooner do we find the winning formula than we lose our star striker. But that's not all. John O'Hara reckons we've got other problems. He would, of course. John's the most miserable kid you've ever met – or are likely to. But for once I think he could have something. It's Carl Bain and Mattie Hughes. Seems they spent most of the presentation ceremony grumbling and backstabbing because they've spent so much of the season on the subs' bench.

A few weeks ago they were getting aggravation off Brain Damage Ramage. Recognize the name? He's Lee Ramage's kid brother. Seems being a scumbag runs in the family. Him and a scabby polecat by the name of Luke Costello have got this gang, and their main purpose in life is to destroy the Diamonds – and me in particular. It's time to re-build. Ronnie's law. Without Davey, our strike force is looking a bit ropey so I might have to partner our other striker Jamie Moore up front. That leaves Miserable John as the most likely candidate to run the midfield. I can't say he'd be my first choice, but until somebody better comes along, he's it. With Carl and Mattie as our remaining cover you can see we're looking pretty thin in the centre. Has John got what it takes? I mean, he's a manic depressive without the ups. Can he rise to the challenge? Will he be able to take the knocks and come back punching?

Will he be anvil or will he be hammer?

Two

Anvil, definitely anvil.

The Tuesday after the awards ceremony there wasn't a trace of self-congratulatory glow left in John O'Hara. So what he'd got his hands on a trophy? So what he'd got his picture in the pink *Echo*? (Back row, third from the left with Daz Kemble's head covering half his face.) None of it mattered after the week-end he'd had.

Friday night he'd discovered a new state of being. Half boy, half ping-pong ball. And Mum and Dad had the bats.

'Like to tell him what you've been up to?' shouted Dad.

'That's rich coming from you,' yelled Mum.

And John? He just sat miserably in the middle of the living room with his eyes glued on the TV screen and his heart being shredded by the two people he loved most in the whole world. Hadn't they ever heard of sparing the kids their problems? John snorted wretchedly. Obviously not. The O'Haras had always had their spats, but the last six months had been a roller coaster ride of rows and sulks. Somehow John had a feeling they were cranking up for the scariest downhill plummet yet. The Big One.

Saturday night they'd discovered a weapon more deadly than the atom bomb, more accurate than an Exocet missile. Silence. John and his big sister Sarah had had to shove pizza round their plates while Mum and Dad trained their freeze guns on each other. The result was two kids caught in the Arctic Zone.

Sunday night Dad wasn't even there. Boys' Night Out or something. Not as though you'd know he was absent. Mum prowled round the house ranting about his misdeeds. Roll on school, John had thought, amazing himself at the idea.

Monday night it was Mum's turn to do a vanishing trick. Governors' meeting at school. And Dad's turn to fling verbal darts at her. 'Governors' meeting,' he'd snarled. 'What does she know about education? Left school with three CSEs and netball certificate.'

Yes, one hell of a week-end. Now John was sitting on a bench, clutching a miniature Union flag he'd made in class and trying to avoid them staring up at him from their places in the school hall. It was Leavers' Assembly and there were Mr and Mrs O'Hara side by side, smiling as sweetly as you like. The model parents. Capital M, capital PUKE. John shuddered. They made him sick.

Then Mrs Harrison was on her feet. Showing off her new hairdo. It was an annual ritual, the Headteacher's end-of-year hairdo. One of these days she'd have a Mohican and make everybody sit up and notice! John allowed himself a smile then turned his attention back to Mrs Harrison, who was thanking everybody for coming. Telling her audience what a lovely Year Six they'd all been. Oh yeah, like she doesn't say that every year. And finally introducing the Leavers' Assembly. The girls on the verge of tears and the boys suppressing smirks of joy at finally escaping Our Lady's Primary. Not that John felt much like smirking. He just wanted the whole thing over, especially the last bit. Mum's bit.

'Welcome to our Leavers' Assembly,' said Melanie Mulcahy, beaming at the audience then curling her top lip over her front teeth to conceal her brace. She was embarrassed about her metallic smile. And the nickname she was struggling to live down – Jaws. 'We have been remembering the teachers who have helped us.'

Helped us, thought John. Sure, like pirates help you walk the plank.

Jacqui Bell was on her feet next, recalling Mrs Willoughby in Reception. 'I put my hand up,' said Ding Dong, 'but she told me to hang on a minute. That was when I threw up all over her shoes.'

Laughter from the parents, especially when Ratso held up a king-sized cartoon of the notorious incident. A rueful smile of recognition from Willoughby the Wallaby. Ah, the joys of teaching. And on it went, right down to their present teacher, Mr May. That's Maggot to most of the boys in his class. Then it was back to the Jaws and Ding Dong show as Melanie and Jacqui screeched out *Memory* on their violins.

'That'll set them off,' whispered Joey Bannen behind him.

And it did. Soon every girl was sobbing her eyes out. But that's what you do at your Leavers' Assembly. A Leavers' Assembly without tears is like a dog without fleas. It's almost a school rule. Only John didn't cry, and neither did his Diamonds team-mates. Not the done thing for the hardest football team on the toughest estate in the north end of Liverpool.

'Nearly finished,' said Daz Kemble under his breath.

'Can't wait,' said Jimmy Mintoe.

He got a glare from Mrs Harrison for that. He went bright red. He hadn't meant it to come out that loudly.

'Thank you, Year Six,' she cooed as the parents' applause subsided. 'But we've got to remember that you're not the only ones who are leaving us.'

Everybody looked at Maggot.

'Mr May is also moving on to pastures new and I would like to ask one of our parent governors …'

John glanced at Mum. Mother turned executioner.

'… One of our parent governors, Mrs O'Hara, to say a few words.'

John's stomach was suddenly playing submarine. Crash dive, crash dive. He watched in an agony of humiliation as Mum walked to the front. The other kids said she was sweet on Maggot. John told them it was a load of rubbish, but it didn't stop them skitting him. And wait until they saw the present Mum had bought for John to bring in on the last day. She couldn't settle for socks or wine or after shave, could she? Not even a *World's Best Teacher* mug. She'd bought him a chess set in its own mahogany box. That would really set the tongues wagging. Tiny needles of shame tormented his skin.

'Mr May has only been at Our Lady's for two years,' she began.

'Two years too long,' hissed Joey.

'But in that time,' Mum continued, 'I have got to know Phillip well.'

'I wonder how well,' whispered Carl Bain.

That made John really squirm. Ever since Mum and Maggot started running the chess club together, he'd had to put up with it. Nudge nudge, wink wink, who does your mum fancy, then?

'He is a marvellous teacher who really looks after the children in his care. He has given up a lot of his own time to coach the school soccer team ...'

'Badly,' commented Daz.

It was true. Despite having the whole Diamonds' side, except for Kev McGovern and Jamie Moore playing for them, they'd had an undistinguished season.

'He has also run a chess club every Wednesday evening.'

With her. It had been the cause of numerous rows with Dad.

'So,' she concluded, 'I would like to thank you on behalf of the whole school and wish you all the best in your new post.'

'Your old lady and Maggot,' said Carl Bain. 'Coo-hoo.'

Shame caught fire and turned to anger.

'Shut your mouth *now*,' said John, 'or I'll shut it for you.'

'Touchy, aren't you?' observed Carl. 'Something *must* be going on.'

John stared straight ahead through the closing music. He watched Mum walking back to her seat. It couldn't be true. It just couldn't.

Three

It was Mum who finally broke the silence on the way home.

'Would you like to tell me what's wrong?' she asked.

John dug himself even deeper into the back seat upholstery. Carl Bain's taunts were still ringing in his ears. 'Nothing.'

'Really?' said Mum. 'Well, I don't want your nothing spoiling my day. I'm going back to the school this evening, and I intend to enjoy myself.'

John noticed Dad's neck stiffen at the mention of school.

'How come?' John asked. 'What are you going back *there* for?'

'I must have told you,' Mum replied, checking the junction at the top of South Parade for oncoming traffic.

'No, you didn't.'

'If you really must know,' Mum told him as she pulled out, 'it's a wine and cheese party for Mr May.'

'I thought you'd already said goodbye to him,' said John.

Dad smiled. My thoughts exactly, he seemed to be saying.

'This is a get-together for the staff,' Mum explained. There was an edge to her voice. Impatience. Maybe something else, too. 'Teachers, governors, PTA, you know the sort of thing.'

'Sounds boring,' said John.

'It would,' said Mum. 'To you everything's boring. Except football, of course.'

Sounds about right, thought John. He was just wondering why Dad was so quiet when the old man finally chipped in.

'So how long's it going to last, this do of yours?'

Mum took a right into Naseby Close and pulled up outside number nine.

'An hour. Two. We might go for a drink afterwards. It depends what the others are doing.'

'Mm.'

John knew Dad's Mms. There was the short Mm, which meant: Good, Fine. Then there was the medium-sized Mm accompanied by a raised eyebrow which meant: Oh really. But this was the extra-long Mm with simmering dark frown. It meant trouble.

'Have you got something to say?' asked Mum.

'Me?' replied Dad, heavy on the sarcasm. 'What could I possibly have to say? You always do what you want anyway.'

John flopped his head back. Couldn't they give it a rest? Just for one day.

'Hello,' said Mum, relieved to change the subject. 'There's our Sarah waiting on the doorstep.' She wound down the window.

'Where's your key, love?'

'Forgot it,' said Sarah. 'I was in a hurry to get out of the house this morning.'

Somebody else who was being heavy on the sarcasm, and John knew why. Mum and Dad had been going at it hammer and tongs over the breakfast table. As per rotten usual. It was all right for Sarah, though. She always had Mr Bean to escape to.

'You must have been there ages,' said Mum.

Sarah was in the Sixth Form at Scarisbrick High and she was usually home by half past two.

'A bit,' Sarah confirmed.

'You'd forget your head if it was loose,' said Dad, marching up the path brandishing his keys.

'You could have popped into Simon's,' said Mum. 'You don't usually need much of an excuse.'

'You mean Beano, don't you?' said John, glad of the chance to tease Sarah. It relieved the tension.

'Don't call him that,' said Sarah.

'Why not?'

'Because I hate it, that's why. Besides, it's cruel.'

So? If Simon didn't want to get skitted he shouldn't have been born with droopy eyelids and a pointy nose. He was Rowan Atkinson to a tee.

'He's gone to Norwich,' said Sarah, ignoring her younger brother.

'Norwich?' Dad repeated, unlocking the front door. 'What's down there?'

'The University of East Anglia,' Sarah answered. 'He's got an interview.'

'University?' scoffed John, 'They're never going to let *him* into a university.' Until that moment he hadn't even realized Sarah's divvy boyfriend had a brain, never mind A levels.

'Cut it out, you,' she snapped, taking a swing at him with her school bag.

'You'll have to be quicker than that,' said John, skipping back.

'I will be,' Sarah warned. 'You wait until you're off your guard.'

'Forget it, sis,' said John. 'I never am.'

The front door slammed behind them. John glanced round.

'I'm going for my shower,' said Mum, jogging upstairs. 'Will you two start tea?' She was speaking to John and Sarah.

'What about me?' asked Dad. 'I'm not helpless, you know.'

Mum gave him a withering look. Another notch on the climb up the roller coaster. As the water in the shower started to run, Dad shrugged his shoulders and dropped into his chair with the *Echo*.

'Come on, pain,' said Sarah, 'you're on turkey burgers, I'll do baked potatoes and salad.'

John nodded and followed her into the kitchen.

'Have they been like that all the way home?' she asked.

'What do you think?'

'Doesn't get any better, does it?'

John shook his head. 'I just hope they patch it up before we go away.'

He'd been looking forward to going on holiday to Lakeland Village for months. It was a new centre in the Lakes. State of the Art swimming pool, cabin in the woods, canoeing, footy coaching every afternoon. Now they were six days away from a brilliant holiday and it looked like Mum and Dad's bickering was going to wreck it.

'Fat chance,' said Sarah gloomily. 'Do you know what Simon calls their marriage? The Lighthouse.'

'Go on,' said John. 'Why?'

'Because it's on and off so much.'

John shook his head. He didn't like being reminded about the times they'd split up. When he was seven, he and Sarah had lived with Mum and Gran for a while. Eventually Dad had turned up with twelve red roses and tickets for a long week-end in London. Expensive sticking plaster, Gran had called it.

Sarah was half-way through chopping the spring onions when she spoke again. 'Did you know that most marriages split up on holiday?' she murmured. 'Then and Christmas are the two worst times.'

That started a horrible retching feeling in John's stomach. It had been happening more and more lately, this wave of sickness whenever Mum and Dad's marriage took another turn for the worse.

'Who told you that?'

'I read it in a magazine.'

'Which one?' asked John. '*Stupids Monthly*? I bet it's not true.'

For a moment Sarah's eyes filled with tears as she remembered the bust-ups over the years, but she recovered well and returned to her chopping. Her reply was still bitter. 'Right now I wouldn't bet against it.'

John wished she'd got him with her school bag. It wouldn't have hurt half as much.

John didn't know what woke him. Footsteps on the landing maybe. Yes, there was somebody there, definitely somebody outside his room. Time to take a look, he thought. Padding across his room, John turned the handle and stepped out.

'Sarah!'

'You didn't half give me a fright,' she said, her breath still shuddering a little.

'I was going to the toilet,' he said, by way of an excuse.

'You sure?'

'Nah, I was having a bit of a nose, to be honest. Wondered who was lurking on the landing.'

'I was nosing too,' said Sarah, wrapping herself tightly in her dressing gown.

'I wanted to know who was mooching about,' said John. 'So what got you up?'

'Mum,' said Sarah. 'She's not back yet.'

John's mind reeled. A feeling like he was pitching forward, falling. 'What time is it?'

'Late,' said Sarah. 'Gone one o'clock. That's a long time for wine and cheese.'

'What about Dad?'

Sarah grimaced. 'Sitting in the living room, building himself up for a row.'

'Great,' said John, a corkscrew turning inside him. 'Next week's going to be fun.'

Sarah sighed.

'You needn't sound so miserable. You're not even coming.'

Sarah smiled. 'The advantages of being eighteen next month. Good luck, little brother.'

'Thanks,' said John as he turned back into his room, his stomach churning. 'I'll need it.'

Four

Yesss! They've done it. Right out of the blue. The league committee have named me for the Liverpool County Cup squad, and there are three more Diamonds players to keep me company. I hadn't even dared hope for a place. This is recognition, at flipping last. This time last year we were the scum of the earth. Now we're flavour of the month. It's the traditional end-of-season tournament, you see. Each of the Liverpool junior leagues picks a team and they play a knock-out. It's a bit like an international really, the best players from teams in each league pitted against each other. Liverpool and Everton usually keep an eye on the competition in the hope of spotting a new Robbie Fowler or Steve Macmanaman. South Sefton haven't won it for five years so we're overdue a good run. There's tough opposition, though. Huyton-with-Roby are the side to beat. They've lifted the silverware the last two years running and they're after a hat trick. It's never been done before.

It'll be weird. Me, Daz, Jamie and Dave playing alongside the likes of Nosmo King and Scott Geraghty. Talk about the best of enemies. But that's footy for you. One minute you're rivals, the next you're comrades in arms. Pull on a different shirt and suddenly you're looking at people in a completely different way. I thought George Rogan and the league committee had passed us over, so I'm thinking: Typical! Picking the blue-eyed boys again. Pot-bellied old divvies. Couldn't recognize soccer talent if it came up and unscrewed their eyeballs. Then I get a phone call off Ronnie Mintoe telling me I'm in, and they're the salt of the earth.

But it'll be an odd experience for another reason.

Dave's last competitive appearance in Sunday league football before his School of Excellence, the last time we *play with Nosmo and Geraghty before they move up to the under-14s. They're a year older than us, you see. Their departure is good news for the Diamonds, of course. Even giving away a big age advantage we won the Challenge Cup this year. Come September we won't be at a disadvantage any more. The older lads will have moved up. The Diamonds will walk it next season and this tournament will be where we announce our intentions.*

Five

The rain was the last straw. It meant John couldn't even escape outside. He'd been watching the fine droplets pock-marking their dustbowl of a garden for half an hour. Wishing it away, begging it to hold off and give him a break. No such luck. It was driving down now, a heavy, drenching downpour. The griping feeling in his guts had begun already.

'It's gone really quiet in there,' he whispered to Sarah as she crossed the kitchen to make a phone call. Mum and Dad had been holed up in the living room for an hour and a half at least.

'I don't know if that's good or bad,' she said. 'Sometimes they seem better after a good old shouting match.'

'Yes,' he replied dubiously. 'Maybe.'

'Anyway,' Sarah said, covering the mouthpiece of the phone with her hand. 'I'm making a call.'

'I'm not stopping you,' John grunted. Now *she* was giving him the heave-ho. Nobody ever had time for him.

'A personal call,' she said. 'To Simon.'

'Oh, Beano.'

Sarah raised an eyebrow. She really hated that nickname. 'So I'd like you to lose yourself.'

'Where? You're in here. They're in the living room.'

'I don't care where,' Sarah said impatiently. 'Just clear off.'

'But ...'

'Go!' Then a sudden change of tone. 'No, not you, Si. I'm talking to our John. Yes ...' A loud laugh. 'Miseryguts.'

John stamped upstairs. Talk about No Hiding Place. He dug his hands in his pockets and made his way along the landing to his room. He stopped outside the door. 'Miseryguts, is it? We'll see about that.' Retracing his steps he crept into Mum and Dad's room. The other extension was in there. Gingerly lifting the phone he listened in on Sarah's conversation. She was asking Beano about his interview.

'It was all right,' Simon told her. 'They asked all the questions I expected. I think I did OK.'

That's when John started his campaign of sabotage, tapping the mouthpiece with his finger.

'What was that?' asked Sarah.

'Dunno.'

The conversation resumed, but not for long. John grabbed a piece of paper from Mum's bedside table and crunched it up next to the mouthpiece.

'Do you think there's a fault on the line?' asked Simon.

'Yes,' said Sarah, 'an obnoxious, spotty one by the name of John O'Hara. GET OFF THE LINE, YOU UGLY LITTLE MORON!'

'Very ladylike,' grumbled John, replacing the phone. He was disappointed. He'd expected the game to last longer, as he escalated to sheep bleating, wolf howls, whoopee-cushion noises, that sort of thing.

'No good at practical jokes, am I?' he grumbled to himself. He caught sight of Mum and Dad's wedding photo on the dressing table and gave a crooked smile. 'Unlike them,' he murmured. 'With their joke marriage.'

Returning to his room, he flopped on his bed and watched the rain streaming down the window panes. It would be bad enough Mum and Dad packing their troubles to bring with them. But what if it was raining as well? That would be the absolute limit. He was coming close to reaching boredom Wharp Factor 5, which is just short of beating your head against the wall, when there was a knock at the door.

'Yes?'

'It's me.'

Sarah.

'Can I come in?'

He opened the door to let her in. Better grovel, he thought, before she batters me. 'Sorry about the phone call.'

'Forget it.'

Come again! Normally, she would have ragged the head off him for that.

'It's Mum and Dad,' she said. 'One of them will be up any time to have a word with you.'

Stomach bubbling. Heart sinking. Going under. Glub, glub, glub.

'What about?'

'What do you think?' said Sarah. 'Them. Their *relationship*.'

They simultaneously stuck their fingers down their throat. They'd got so used to their parents on-and-off marriage they had a set of stock replies to the latest shennanigans. Hands covering eyes at the mention of the word *love*, fake nose-picking if they held hands or got smoochy, finger down the throat if they talked about their relationship, new start, making a go of it or taking a long look at themselves in the mirror. John and Sarah were still giggling when Dad popped his head round the door.

'You two sound happy.'

'It's called good acting, Dad,' said Sarah pointedly. 'We deserve an Oscar.'

John marvelled at her cockiness. He would never have dared attempt such a blatant put-down.

'I'm going round Simon's.'

'OK,' said Dad. 'See you later.'

'If I don't see you first.'

John had discovered a new word for his sister. Feisty. Particularly when she'd insisted on staying home instead of joining the family holiday. Dad would have said she was being downright rude.

'She's on good form today.'

John scratched his nose. 'Yes.'

'I came up to have a word.'

Just one? That would be a novelty.

'Yes.'

'About me and your mum.'

Obviously.

'Yes.'

'We've been going through a bit of a rough patch.'

'No-o-o,' said John in mock surprise. Why let Sarah have all the good lines?

'Are you trying to be funny, son?'

Trying, thought John, but obviously not succeeding.

'No.'

'Anyway, we've had a good old heart-to-heart.'

So what's new? That's the way it went. Emotional meltdown then heart-to-heart, then repeat the whole thing over again.

'And we've decided to make a real effort to have a good summer.'

Dad gave John a long stare. 'Are you listening to me?'

'Yes, you're going to make an effort.'

Dad ignored the sceptical reception his announcement was getting. 'That's right, starting with the holiday. It's going to be a new start, just you see.'

John picked at a loose thread on his duvet cover.

'Is that OK?'

'Sure, whatever.'

But as Dad walked out of the room, John found himself sticking his finger back down his throat. This time the gagging was for real.

A new start, eh.

Now would that be the sixteenth or the seventeenth?

Six

'Hang on there, John.'

It was Dave and Jimmy. As he turned to wait for them, they play-fought along the pavement. Somebody was happy that sultry Thursday morning.

'What's up with you?' John asked. 'Won the Lottery or something?'

'Or something,' said Dave. 'Tell him, Jim.'

'Guess how many of our lads are in the South Sefton side this Sunday.'

'Two,' said John off-handedly.

'Two,' scoffed Jimmy. 'It's four. Trust you to guess too low.'

Actually, John had expected the big zero but he'd been trying to sound upbeat.

'Yes,' said Dave. 'You need to lighten up, John.'

'That the best advice you can come up with?' sneered John. 'Be a light bulb?'

'Which side of the bed did you get out of this morning?' asked Jimmy.

John shook his head and walked on. 'Go on,' he said with all the enthusiasm of a mud pie. 'Who's in the team?'

'It's not the final side,' said Dave. 'Just a squad of sixteen. They'll pick the final eleven from it later. There's me ...'

'Naturally,' said John. He liked Dave, but that didn't mean he wasn't a bit jealous. After all, this was the jammy beggar who'd got himself on Everton's books.

'Jamie, Daz and ...'

'Wait for it,' Jimmy interrupted.

'Guv.'

'Guv!' John stared in disbelief. 'They'll never pick him.'

'Why not?' asked Dave. 'He's in there with a shout.'

'There'd be murder,' said John. 'He makes enough waves in our league. Imagine what he'll be like playing kids from the south end. He thinks anybody who lives south of Walton is a woollyback.'

'That's nothing,' said Dave. 'He thinks anyone from outside of Liverpool is a flipping alien.'

'It's good, though, isn't it?' asked Jimmy. 'Four Diamonds out of a squad of sixteen. Uncle Ronnie's over the moon. It wouldn't have happened if Gord's dad was still managing us.'

'So when are the matches being played?' asked John. 'I'd like to watch.'

'You better had,' said Jimmy. 'Guv says it's a three line whip. If you don't get along to cheer the lads you're the one who'll get the whip.'

'The semis are this Sunday,' said Dave. 'We've drawn the Aigburth and Wavertree League.'

'That good?' asked John.

'Could be worse,' said Jimmy. 'At least we've avoided Huyton. They're the business.'

They'd reached the school gates. Just a few more days and they would be free.

'So I can tell Guv you'll be there?' asked Jimmy.

'I'll do my best,' said John. 'But we go on holiday on Sunday.'

'You mean you're not willing to give up your holiday for the Diamonds?' said Dave in mock-horror.

'I think we're going late,' said John, ignoring the comment. 'If I can get away, I'll come.'

'I wouldn't like to be in your shoes if you don't,' said Dave, only half joking. 'Guv wouldn't be happy.'

'And don't forget,' said Jimmy. 'Uncle Ron and Guv are looking to make changes in the team. Re-building.'

'They wouldn't drop me,' said John, a note of panic entering his voice. 'Not for going on holiday.'

Jimmy smiled. He was one of the nice guys of the team, but even he couldn't resist taking a rise out of old Miseryguts. 'You never know, John lad, you never know.'

The words came out as a joke, but John wasn't so sure. Not with his luck.

'Won't you be cutting it fine?' asked Mum.

'No way,' John replied. 'We can't arrive at the place until four o'clock. There's loads of time for me to watch the lads play.'

'But the packing ...'

John was ahead of her on that one, too.

'You know you always have it done days in advance.'

'That important, is it?'

John thought of Kev and keeping his place in the Diamonds.

'Definitely. So can I?'

'So long as your dad will run you in the car. I'll check with him.'

'Wouldn't you rather I asked him?'

Mum frowned. 'Meaning?'

John felt embarrassed. 'I just meant ...'

'I know what you meant. There's no need to worry, John. Everything's fine. Didn't your dad tell you we'd patched things up?'

'Yes, but ...'

'This holiday is going to be a new start and that's a promise.'

John looked into Mum's round, smiling face and he trusted her. No fingers down the back of the throat. He trusted her.

It was a promise. And you don't break promises.

Seven

'Listen up, lads,' said George Rogan. 'Here's the team.'

Kev looked around the changing-room. All his old rivals were there: Nosmo, Scott Geraghty, Kenny Mason, Skinhead. He found himself holding his breath.

'In goal, Daz Kemble ...'

'Yiss!'

'Nice to see such enthusiasm, Kevin,' said George. 'But let me finish. The back four is Ged Lawrence, John King, Terry Frost and Michael Rathbone.'

Nosmo was smiling broadly. Two Longmoor players in the side already. Still, they *were* champions.

'Midfield,' George continued.

This was it.

'Kenny Mason, Scott Geraghty ...'

Both the Ajax midfielders. Kev couldn't believe it.

'Greg Wilson ...'

'Who?'

Nosmo grinned. 'He means Skinhead, you div.'

Another Longmoor player.

'And,' said George, ignoring the interruption. 'Adrian Jones.'

Kev barely listened to the rest of the team. He was gutted. Dave Lafferty was in, but that wasn't much consolation.

'Aw, what's up, McGovern?' sneered Nosmo. 'Disappointed?'

'Drop dead, Nos,' Kev retorted.

But there was one more disappointment. George handed Nosmo the captain's armband.

So this is how South Sefton lined up against Aigburth, playing 4–4–2:

Daz Kemble
(Rough Diamonds)

Ged Lawrence (St Patrick's Thistle)	John 'Nosmo' King (Longmoor Celtic)	Terry Frost (St Bede's)	Mick Rathbone (Longmoor Celtic)
Kenny Mason (Ajax Aintree)	Scott Geraghty (Ajax Aintree)	Greg 'Skinhead' Wilson (Longmoor Celtic)	Adrian Jones (Northend United)
	Craig Lennox (Ajax Aintree)	Dave Lafferty (Rough Diamonds)	

Kev trailed out of the changing-rooms and took his place on the bench with the other subs. He sat with his head bowed. It wasn't lost on his watching mates.

'I don't know why he's so down in the mouth,' said Ant. 'There are two of our lads playing. That's not bad.'

'Come off it, Ant,' said John. 'Since when was Guv satisfied with *not bad*?'

Ant nodded slowly. Old Miseryguts had a point there.

'They're ready to kick off,' said Joey Bannen, before launching an ear-piercing screech. 'Come on Sef-ton!'

South Sefton were wearing Inter Milan colours, blue and black stripes. Aigburth were in all white.

'Sefton, Sefton, Sefton,' Joey was chanting shrilly.

The refrain was taken up by the rest of the local spectators. Unfortunately, it didn't seem to inspire the home side. Within five minutes South Sefton were on the back foot and Aigburth were raiding at will down the channels. It looked like a massacre in the making.

'Get a grip, Sefton,' yelled Ant. 'You're getting pulled all over the place. Call yourself a captain, Nosmo?'

'You can tell they've never played together,' said John's dad.

'I know,' said John. 'There's no shape to the side.'

'They would have been better putting the Diamonds on,' said Dad. 'All eleven of you.'

John smiled. 'I think you're a bit biased, Dad.'

A moment later the smile vanished from his face. He'd spotted Carl and Mattie and they were moving in his direction.

'Oh, come on, Sefton,' groaned Ratso loudly. 'Get a flipping grip.'

But it was Aigburth who had a grip – on their opponent's throat. Their wingers had the beating of Ged Lawrence and Mick Rathbone and their crosses were causing havoc in the Sefton penalty area. Twice they came close with headers. Fortunately Daz was on good form, palming them over.

Just along the touch line Kev had woken up from his sulk. 'Go to 'em,' he was shouting. 'Nosmo, push up. You're defending too deep.'

Nosmo didn't welcome this advice. 'Since when were you the skipper?' he shouted back. 'I'm wearing the armband, not you, McGovern.'

Kev shook his head.

'Guv's right,' said Bashir. 'Sefton have to come out and get in a tackle.'

Carl sneered. 'Listen to him,' he said loudly. 'Only been over here two minutes and he's telling us how to play our game.'

Bashir's eyes flashed angrily. He was one of the few black kids in the South Sefton league and he was used to jibes like that from the opposition, but not from a team-mate.

'Bash is right,' said John, keen to get in a dig at Carl. 'So quit bad-mouthing him.'

Another sneer from Carl. 'Who rattled your cage?'

'Now, now,' said Dad. 'Let's not quarrel, lads.'

Sefton had steadied the ship a bit and Dave Lafferty and Craig Lennox were at last getting some service up front. Dave came close with a bicycle kick and Craig almost bundled in a long, looping corner from Kenny Mason. Just when Sefton looked like hanging on to a flattering nil-all scoreline until half-time, Aigburth struck. Ady Jones lost the ball in midfield. Some neat inter-passing at speed put one of the Aigburth strikers clear and he side-footed it past Daz for the opening goal.

'That's torn it,' said Ant.

'Bad time to concede a goal,' said Jimmy as the ref blew for the interval.

John was listening to the instant analysis merchants when Dad tapped him on the shoulder. 'I'm just going for a wander,' he said. 'Get me a coffee from that refreshment stall, son. Buy yourself something out of this.'

John took the fiver his dad was holding out and headed for the queue.

'How come you're here, anyway?' asked Carl, joining the queue a couple of people behind John. 'I thought you were on holiday.'

'Who told you that?'

'Jimmy. Why, is it another of your secrets?'

John despised the sly smile that spread across Carl's face.

'This afternoon,' he said.

'Taking any teachers along with you?' asked Carl, unable to resist the dig.

John ignored him.

'Where are you going, anyway?' asked Carl. 'We're off to that new Lakeland place this afternoon.'

John snapped round. '*You* are! But that's where we're going.'

'Never!'

'Yes, we've had it booked for months.'

Carl frowned, not sure what to make of the news. 'Mum got us a late booking two weeks ago. Cancellation, or something. How long are you there for?'

'A week.'

'Same as us.'

There was an uncomfortable silence. Mattie joined them. 'Something the matter?' he asked.

'We're going to same place on holiday,' said Carl. 'Bit of a coincidence, isn't it?'

Yes, thought John as he scanned the small crowd for Dad. A big one. He bought Dad's coffee and a can of Coke for himself and walked past Carl and Mattie. Any other time he would have been glad of their silence, but he was feeling anxious.

'I'm going to find my dad,' said John.

He tracked him down making his way back across the field.

'Three-nil to Huyton in the other semi,' he informed John.

'That what you've been doing?' asked John. 'Checking out the other teams?'

Dad took the plastic cup and sipped his coffee. 'Among other things.'

Not five spaces away, and watching them intently, stood Carl's mum.

'The second half can't be as bad as the first,' said Kev. He'd come off the subs' bench to have a word with the rest of the Diamonds.

'Don't bet on it,' said John, arriving ahead of his dad.

'You'd better lose that attitude,' said Kev. 'I've got plans for you.'

'Plans,' stammered John anxiously. 'What plans?'

'Just plans. I'll be having a word soon.'

'But …'

'Soon,' Kev insisted. 'Soon.'

'Are they making any changes, Guv?' asked Ratso.

Kev shook his head.

'Do they want to win this, or what?' asked Ant.

'Don't ask me,' said Kev. 'Looks like I'm just here to make up the numbers. They don't want somebody with fire in their belly.'

'You'll get a game,' said Bashir.

'Yes,' said Joey, 'especially if it stays like this.'

John was hardly listening. His mind was spinning. First there was Dad going walkabout. The holiday was a new start, that's what Mum had said. She'd *promised*. Didn't the promise go for Dad, too? Then there were Guv's mysterious plans for him. Fear gripped him like a claw.

'Anyway,' said Kev, 'I'd better go back over there. You never know. See you later, lads.'

'Yes, see you, Guv,' they chorused chirpily.

'See you,' said John uncertainly.

Within minutes of the re-start Sefton had slipped further behind.

Ady Jones had committed himself to a tackle in the last third and been sold the dummy. The Aigburth player had run on and put a team-mate clear. From five yards, putting the ball past Daz was a formality.

'Where's my cover?' Daz bawled, striding towards Nosmo. 'Have I got to do this all by myself, or what?'

'Good old Daz,' said Jimmy. 'Always so even-tempered.'

Nosmo tried to shrug the furious keeper away and accidentally caught him in the face with his elbow. Daz reacted angrily. It was only the intervention of Scott Geraghty that prevented a fight.

'You Diamonds,' snarled Nosmo. 'Always looking for a fight.'

'A bit of fight wouldn't do this shower any harm,' observed Ant.

The Sefton coaching staff must have come to the same conclusion. Before play could resume there was a double substitution. Off came Ady Jones who'd had a shocker and Skinhead who'd made no impression on a well-organized Aigburth defence.

'Who's coming on?' asked Ratso.

'Guess,' said Jimmy.

Kev and Jamie were limbering up excitedly to their left.

'More like it,' said Gord. 'Diamonds to the rescue.'

John would have loved to join in the excited talk, but he found himself searching for Carl. He couldn't keep his mind on the match.

'Looking for someone, son?' asked Dad.

'Yes,' said John, deciding to test him. 'I can't see Carl.'

Sure enough, Dad's expression changed.

'What's going on, Dad?'

Dad looked uncomfortable. 'Come over here,' he said. 'I don't want people sticking their noses in.'

Glancing back at the pitch where Kev was already getting stuck in, John followed.

'I think I'm missing something, John,' said Dad. 'What's all this about young Carl?'

'You were talking to his mum.'

'No, I wasn't. Anyway, what if I had been?'

'It's supposed to be a new start, Dad. The holiday. You and Mum.' He felt stupid. The words were spilling out in a sort of shorthand and they made no sense. Had he been imagining it, after all?

'That's right,' said Dad. 'That's it exactly. A new start. Everything's going to be fine. You're worrying about nothing. Come on, let's get back to that match.'

The game was very different to the one they'd left a few minutes earlier. Suddenly the midfield area was being keenly contested.

'How's it going?' asked John.

'Guv's made all the difference,' said Ant.

'Nosmo doesn't like it, though,' said Jimmy. 'Kev's giving the orders.'

As if to prove the point Kev dispossessed his man and drove forward. 'Make space,' he yelled. 'Don't bunch together, you divs.' He was waving players frantically forward. 'Move yourselves.'

Dave was the first to respond, making a diagonal run into the box. Spotting him, Kev chipped the ball forward. Rising from a standing start, Dave nodded the ball into Craig Lennox's path. Craig kept his cool and rolled the ball under the keeper's body.

'Two-one,' said John, his spirits reviving after the little chat. 'We're back in contention. Think we can do it, Dad?'

'So long as McGovern keeps playing the way he is, I'd say it's a cert.'

John beamed. He felt so grateful to his dad. Grateful for giving him his life back.

Five minutes later, Kev was in the thick of the action again. Seizing on a poor pass out by the Aigburth centreback, he knocked it left-side to Jamie. Going past his marker Jamie hit the ball low and hard across the goalmouth. It was Dave's boot that met the cross. Two-all.

'Go for it, lads,' yelled John. 'They're there for the taking.'

Kev didn't need any encouragement. In the last ten

minutes he carved the Aigburth defence open three times. Jamie was unlucky to hit the woodwork with the first chance, but the other two chances found the net as Dave recorded his hat trick. He celebrated the third goal with a neat backwards flip.

'Four-two,' said John excitedly. 'Anybody know how the other match went on?'

'I've just been over there,' said Ratso. 'Eight-nil to Huyton. They're going to take some beating.'

'We'll do it, won't we, Dad?' asked John.

'With a bit of luck. Anyway, we'd better make a move, son.'

'Yes,' said John, I'll see you all next week for the final.'

'Yes, see you, John. Have a good time.'

Kev and Dave had just arrived from their triumph on the field. 'And that's an order, Miseryguts.'

John joined in the laughter.

As they reached Jacob's Lane car park, John looked up at his dad.

'It's going to be a great holiday, isn't it, Dad?'

'Definitely,' said Dad. 'And that's a promise.'

Eight

Nothing could dampen John's spirits on the way back. He wouldn't allow it to. There was a tightness in his chest; he was almost dizzy with happiness. He'd had a scare, a big one, and now he wanted to be happy. He *would* be happy. Dad had told him what he'd wanted to hear and he was determined to believe it, no matter what. Watching Guv working his magic on the pitch, he'd come to a conclusion. There are two sorts of people in the world: the ones who do things and the ones who have things done to them. While Guv had always been a doer, John was definitely done to. Done to by Mum, done to by Dad, done to by other kids. But now he felt strong. If Guv could wish things different and make them so, then he could, too.

John was desperate for his family to be like the ones he saw on the telly. Two scrubbed smiling adults, two scrubbed smiling kids – one boy, one girl. The O'Haras were perfect. They had the right number of individuals, the right sort of house, the right sort of car. In Diamond estate terms, they were positively rich. All they needed was the right sort of happiness. Which was exactly what they were going to have. He had decided. He, John O'Hara, had decided it and it was going to happen. Even the sight of Costello, Brain Damage and Co, the estate bullies, hanging round South Parade didn't faze him too much.

Dad saw him craning to see what they were up to. 'Something wrong, John?'

John spied the gang's quarry. It was Carl and Mattie. The gang had cornered them outside the bookies. More pressure to break with the Diamonds. John had a feeling it wouldn't take much.

'John,' his father repeated, 'is there something the matter?'

'What?'

John saw that Mrs Bain had caught up with Carl, and the gang were moving away. She was obviously giving them a piece of her mind.

'You look like something's bothering you.'

'Oh no,' John replied hurriedly, not wanting to spoil things by mentioning Carl or his mum. 'Just a few of the lads, that's all.'

'I bet they wish *they* were off to Lakeland,' said Dad.

'Yes,' said John. Don't mention Carl, he told himself. And, whatever you do, don't mention his mum. 'I bet they do.'

The stormy rain showers of earlier in the week had given way to blue skies and dazzling sunshine. Everything seemed to be picking up.

'You know what we could do when we get in,' said Dad.

The group on South Parade were out of sight. And quite quickly out of mind. John wanted to keep it that way.

'What's that, Dad?'

'Phone Lakeland. In the brochure it says you can book activities in advance. I'm going to have a go at wind-surfing. You?'

'Footy coaching, of course.'

'Yes,' said Dad, 'but that's only one day.'

'No,' said John. 'Every day. Yet get a thirty per cent discount. It's in the special offers on the last page.'

'Been making plans, have you?'

John chuckled. 'Of course.'

'Anything else?'

'They've got laser clay shooting. Do you think I'm old enough?'

'No harm in asking,' said Dad. 'You know, something tells me this is gong to be a great holiday.'

'You look pleased with yourself,' said Sarah as John walked into the kitchen. There was a spring in his step.

'What's wrong with that?' he said brightly. 'We are off on holiday.' He looked at Sarah and Beano, who was standing next to her. 'Present company excepted.'

'I can't say I'm shedding any tears,' said Sarah. 'I remember all the other ones we've had. Ugh.'

'Behave,' said John. 'Didn't you read the brochure? It looks brilliant.' He knew he was gushing, but if you're going to will things better you have to work at it. He wasn't about to let Sarah break the spell.

'I didn't mean Lakeland,' said Sarah, glancing down the hallway for any sign of Mum or Dad. 'There's nothing wrong with the place. I meant *them*. They'd put the mockers on Paradise.'

'No,' said John excitedly. 'It's all right. They're going to make a new start. They promised.'

'Oh,' said Beano sceptically, 'like it isn't the first time.'

'Who asked you to chip in?' snapped John. 'This is none of your business.'

Beano shrugged his shoulders which irritated John even more. They never had taken to each other. Little wonder, really. Beano didn't even like football. Tennis was his game. Figured.

'Simon's right,' said Sarah softly. 'I know you're excited, John, and I hope everything does turn out OK. I really do want you to have a good holiday. It's just …'

'Yes, go on, say it.'

'Don't go building your hopes up.' She glanced at Beano. A look which said: Leave this to me. 'I've been here before remember. Many times. Promises are cheap. I've heard them all.'

'But what if it's different?' demanded John, willing it to be. 'What if they really mean it?'

'Then everyone lives happily ever afterwards,' said Beano, unable to conceal the sneering tone in his voice.

John darted a hostile glance in his direction then leaned against the kitchen surface. 'Why are you doing this,

Sarah?' he asked. 'Just because you don't want to go. Why've you got to spoil it for me?'

'That isn't the idea,' she replied. 'It really isn't. I just don't want to see you hurt.' She hesitated. 'They've both been seeing other people, you know. That's how bad it's got.'

John put his hands over his ears, then realizing how stupid he must look he jabbed a finger at her. 'You're making it up,' he shouted. 'You and that meff.'

'John!'

That's when Mum made an entrance. 'What's all the shouting in aid of ?' she asked.

Sarah lowered her eyes. 'Nothing, Mum.'

'Nothing, eh?' said Mum. 'Sounded like a pretty heated nothing from where I was standing.'

John knew Mum would go ballistic if she found out what Sarah had told him, and a row was the last thing he needed just then. Swallowing his pride, he dived in first. 'She was telling me off for having a go at Beano.'

'That all?' asked Mum.

'Yes,' said Sarah. 'That's about it.'

'Then we'd better get ready,' said Mum. 'There's less than an hour to check we haven't forgotten anything.'

John started to follow her out of the kitchen.

'John,' said Sarah.

'What is it now?'

'It's about the promises,' she said. 'People do break them, you know.'

Nine

I nearly didn't make it. I was gutted when I didn't make the South Sefton final eleven, but it worked out all right in the end. More by luck than good management, of course. What would you do with Nosmo and the rest of them? They're more interested in scoring points off us Diamonds than making sure the team win. Talk about cutting your nose off to spite your face. Anyway, I'm not going to let it faze me. I'll do anything to get us playing as a unit. Will it work? Who knows? There are a lot of old scores to settle. All I know is we've got to give it a go. There's a long summer ahead and I need a few footy memories to keep me going through it.

It's the Saturdays when you start to feel it. It's like a hunger – the absence of football. No preview on the telly, no sitting with your ear glued to Radio City, no results service at tea-time. No Gary Lineker, no Alan Hansen, no Andy Gray. Saturdays in summer are total non-days. Sunday mornings are just as bad. You wake up empty inside. No nicking the paper off Mum to read the footy section, no talking to the lads about the Blues' performance on the way to Jacob's Lane. No arguing about the rights and wrongs of the latest transfer deals. Worst of all, no match of our own to go to. I haven't even been through the first footy-less Saturday yet and I'm dreading it already. Next Sunday's junior league final against Huyton is the last game of the summer. After that it's downhill all the way.

I started feeling this way right after the game. O'Hara set me off talking about his holidays. It made me realize other kids have got something in their lives besides football. John and Carl are going away. Next Monday it's Daz and Joey's turn. They're off to Spain. That's right, the Kembles are taking Joey along so Daz has got a mate to knock around with. Most of the others are going away somewhere. Gord, the jammy get, he's off to Disney.

They thought it was off a couple of months back when his dad had trouble at work, but his mum got a new job so it's back on. Worst of all, Dave Lafferty is playing cricket until autumn. Sounds like heresy to me, but how can you argue with our most successful player? That leaves yours truly kicking his heels on the streets of the Diamond along with the rest of the stay-at-home brigade. That's Ratso, Ant, Jamie and Bashir. Bashir keeps saying he's got a special reason for staying on the Diamond, which he can't tell us about. Personally, I think his family is as skint as mine and he's too proud to admit it, but we'll see. I haven't had a holiday away since my parents split. Mum's scraping round for coppers as per usual and Dad hasn't shown up for weeks. No wonder I have so much time to think about re-building the team for next season!

So let's forget about holidays. Here are my thoughts on the team. If Sunday's match against Aigburth confirmed one thing, it's that the Diamonds need me up front. Dave scored a brilliant hat trick. He'll be missed. It's not that Jamie isn't a good goal-poacher. He is. Two good feet and a predator's instinct. What he's lacking is Dave's ability to hold the ball up, to intimidate defenders. Jamie's just too lightweight for that. We've tried him as a lone striker and he just faded out of the game. He needs somebody alongside him who'll mix it with the opposition defence, take the beat off him and create the openings. Me, in other words. But that leaves us with John and Ratso in the middle of the park, and that has me worried. Even if we keep Carl and Mattie and move one of them into a three-man midfield, it looks lightweight. One of them has to do my job and be the powerhouse. It's no use asking Ratso to do it. He's skilful and he's got a heart like a lion, but unfortunately he was born with the build of an *anorexic stick insect. Carl and Mattie are too slow, too selfish and too lacking in ability to hack it. That's even if they stick with the Diamonds, which seems doubtful.*

That leaves the player I've had pencilled in ever since I found out Dave was leaving us. I'm talking about John, of course. I have to confess I wasn't sure he had the commitment to the Diamonds. As for his temperament, he always seemed ready to give up at the first setback. I've lost count of the number of times when we've gone a goal down and he's been ready to throw his hand in. He's surprised me just lately, though. He seemed like a different kid at the match. Looks like John's the man for the job.

PART TWO

Promises Broken

One

If there's a Heaven, John thought as he freewheeled down the steep path between the pines, this is what it must be like. Two days into the holiday, Sarah's dire warning was a distant memory. Their accommodation was a cabin by a stream. You don't get that in Liverpool, your own private stream. Transport round the village was a hired mountain bike. Cars are banned so Mum and Dad had given him total freedom. All he had to say was: 'I'm off out.' They even gave him a few quid a day so he could get a sandwich or a pizza from the village centre. No lectures about the traffic, because there was none. No being back for a set time, because they were working to the good old Western clock. Sun-up till sun-down. Brilliant. They trusted him. Even better, without Sarah to shoot down his hopes every two minutes, he trusted them.

One morning he'd got up at seven o'clock just to be out and about while everyone else was sleeping. He'd heard that there were lizards living in an old stone wall on the other side of the stream. There were, and all. He'd never seen one outside Chester Zoo. The only wildlife on the Diamond were packs of wild dogs and packs of even wilder kids. He'd been so excited at discovering his first reptile he'd run back to the cabin with it and burst into his parents' room. Then the daft little beggar jumped out of his hand, got itself lost in the duvet and took ten minutes to find. Mum was hysterical and Dad was in angry mourning for his lost lie-in. That was the only telling off he'd had in two days, though. Best of all, he'd hardly seen Carl. One glimpse on the rapids in the pool and a couple of minutes standing behind him in the queue for table tennis. He could live with that.

'Morning, son,' said one of the security guards.

In Liverpool, security guards are fellers in black trousers and white shirts who glare at you if you go into a shop without your parents. In Lakeland they wear khaki shorts, smile and say good morning. Like adopted uncles with shades.

'Morning,' chirped John.

It was nice to say good morning to people.

At the bottom of the slope he started to pedal again to keep up the momentum on the climb to the Sports Hall. His second footy coaching session started in ten minutes on the astro turf.

'John!'

Somebody was shouting at him.

'John!'

'Oh, hi there, Mum.'

'Have you seen your dad anywhere?'

'No.'

She was frowning, but he didn't pay much attention.

'I've lost track of him,' she said. 'Still, he'll turn up.'

John smiled. 'He usually does.'

'Yes,' said Mum, frowning harder. 'Usually.'

The loaded way she said *usually* rang alarm bells, but only for a moment. Footy practice was calling.

'I've got to get off,' said John.

'OK,' said Mum. 'See you later. I'm going to try aromatherapy.'

'What's that?'

'Massage with smellies,' she answered.

John grimaced. It sounded disgusting.

'At least, that's what I think it is.'

'Good luck,' said John.

'See you later.'

John waved and re-started the climb. It was an effort after having stopped and he had to lift himself out of his saddle to make it. It was worth it. From the top of the hill he could see the grey-green hills stretching into the shimmering heat haze. Heaven. He'd woken up in Heaven. At least, that's what he thought until he saw Carl padlocking his bike. You don't get divvies like him in Heaven.

'What are you here for?' John asked.

'Same as you. Footy coaching.'

'I don't know why you bother,' said John acidly. 'You never get off the subs' bench back home.'

'So whose fault's that?' asked Carl. 'Ronnie flipping Mintoe and that plank McGovern. They think they're big, being manager and captain, but they're not – they're just stupid. They've got it in for me and Mattie.'

'Conspiracy, is it?'

'You bet it is. Just because we trod on Gord's toes one time.'

John remembered the way Carl and Mattie ganged up on Gord. They did a lot more than tread on the guy's toes; they had him thinking he was the lowest form of life, a real Billy-No-Mates.

'Couldn't be that you're no good, then?' he asked.

Carl could give it but he certainly couldn't take it. 'Shut it, O'Hara.'

'Make me,' said John. 'You're on your own here. There's no Mattie to back you up.'

Carl squared up for an instant, then seemed to think better of it. In the end, he simply shook his head and set off towards the astro turf. 'If you're so rotten good, show me where it matters. On the pitch.'

'Glad to,' said John. He was no Dave Lafferty or Kev McGovern, but he could take that moron with his legs bound together.

When they arrived, their soccer coach Colin was already there, setting out the plastic cones.

'Good morning, lads,' he said in his thick Geordie accent.

'Hi, Colin,' said John.

Using the coach's first name was John's way of telling Carl he already knew the ropes and that the newcomer was an intruder.

'We'll give the rest five minutes or so,' said Colin. 'So what's your name?'

'Carl.'

'Uh oh, another scouser, eh? Whereabouts in Liverpool are you from, Carl? I was at John Moores University. Had a little flat off Ullet Road.'

'I'm from the north end,' said Carl. 'The Diamond, same as him.'

'Mates, are you?'

Carl glared at John. 'We know each other.'

Hearing the frostiness in Carl's voice, Colin decided to leave well alone.

'How many customers have I got now?' he wondered aloud. 'Thirteen, is it? That'll do.'

The session started with a dribbling and tackling exercise. John immediately opted for Carl's group and went in hard. He saw Colin watching him.

'OK, boys,' he said. 'Get into pairs. Dribble and tackle. Whoever loses the ball is out. This is an eliminator, right. Last one standing wins. And by the way …' he looked pointedly at John, 'no rough stuff. This is fun, remember. You're on holiday.'

But John could still hear Carl and Mattie's taunts. Malice doesn't take a break, and neither would his revenge.

'You and me,' he told Carl. 'Call it a duel.'

'Suits me,' said Carl.

But it was an uneven battle. It wasn't for nothing that Carl had sat out the season on the bench. It wasn't that he didn't have the temperament for football. There was aggression a-plenty in his character. It was skill that lacked. He had all the natural footballing talent of a Galapagos tortoise. John dispossessed him easily and went on to the next partner. He got down to the last pair, a big lad from Middlesbrough in a Looney Toons T-shirt. He looked thirteen if he was a day, and he was good. When he wrapped a leg round John's and came away with the ball, Carl expressed his satisfaction by clapping sarcastically.

'Nice one, O'Hara. I suppose Maggot taught you that move. Teaches your family a lot, I hear.'

Typical of Carl. He just couldn't leave it alone. The blood was beating behind John's eyes, but seeing Colin watching them closely he bit his tongue. A moment later, sidling unseen up to Carl, he hissed his answer.

'Cut out the cracks about Maggot or I'll burst you. I told you it isn't true.'

Carl had his answer all worked out. 'That's all right, O'Hara. It doesn't bother me if you want to kid yourself.'

'Take it back!'

'No way.'

'Then the duel's still on,' said John. 'Last man standing.'

—— 47 ——

Carl nodded.

Next up was a game ideal for their purpose.

'The odd numbers will come in handy,' said Colin. 'Looney Toons, you go in goal. The rest of you line up over there.'

You had to run in competition with a player from the opposing team. Race to first base, touch, back to the line. Race to second base, touch, back to the line. Race for the ball. Advance on the keeper resisting your opponent's tackles. Score. Six boys in each team. Best out of six wins.

'OK, boys,' said Colin. 'Get ready.'

John and Carl had one thought in their minds. The duel. Last man standing. They jockeyed in their lines until they were up against each other.

'Scousers next, eh?' said Colin, trying against all odds to keep things light-hearted. 'Better have my red card available.'

John's side were two-nil down and desperately needed to score.

'On your marks, set, go,' shouted Colin. 'Cheer them on, teams.'

Carl had gone early and was first to the base, but by the time they were going for the ball, John was a couple of strides clear. Steering the ball to the right, he coaxed the goalie out. With Carl struggling to make up ground John had little difficulty slotting the ball home. It did nothing for his team, who ended up losing the game four-two. It hardly seemed to matter, even when Colin declared a forfeit. The losers had to do press-ups. Or, as Colin put it: 'Drop and give me twenty!'

John would have given 100. He'd won the second round of the duel with lame-brain Bain.

'Once more,' said Colin, 'then we'll have a match.'

'About time,' shouted Looney Toons. He wasn't happy about being exiled in goal.

Again John and Carl faced one another, and again it was John who came off best. But this time Carl wasn't prepared to flounder in his wake. He stuck out a leg and brought John down.

'Are you all right, John?' asked Colin.

'Yes.'

But he wasn't. He'd fallen awkwardly and was wincing with pain.

'Is it your ankle?'

John nodded.

'I think you'd better sit out the match,' said Colin. 'Just in case. I'll take a look at you in a few minutes. We'll go over to first aid if it's still giving you gip.'

The Diamonds' code was to carry on regardless. As Guv used to say: don't come crying to me unless your head's hanging off or you're dead. Except John's ankle was telling him a different tale.

'I'll sit it out,' he said.

He couldn't do a thing about Carl mouthing *wimp* at him. Then, much to John's disgust, Carl's team won eight-five.

'How's that ankle?' asked Colin.

'Better,' said John. 'I'll be back tomorrow.'

As he limped back towards his bike, Carl jogged past. 'I'll see you then, O'Hara. Last man standing.'

'Yes,' said John, itching to put him in his place. 'Last man standing.'

Two

It was a hot, clammy Wednesday afternoon when Ratso suggested taking a look at a possible new addition to the Diamonds. Nobody was arguing. The boys were bored. They'd been hanging round South Parade watching the shopfitters working on number seventeen.

'I tell you,' said Ratso. 'This lad's good.'

'What's his name again?' asked Kev.

'Dunno. He's got some engine on him, though. He was everywhere the time I saw him last week. I've never seen anybody cover so much grass in a game.'

'And he'll definitely be there?'

'So he said. Down the rec most days. Nothing else to do.'

'So where's Bashir?' asked Ant. 'I'm bored stiff hanging round here.' Which was a bit rich seeing as they'd only been there five minutes.

'He'll be here soon,' said Kev.

'I hope so,' said Ant. 'I want to see this discovery of Ratso's. We don't half need a replacement for Dave.'

'Do you reckon Bashir really has got something big to tell us?' asked Ratso.

'Nah,' said Ant. 'Just talk.'

South Parade was a small, bleak shopping precinct built in the sixties. Over the years there had been talk of a cinema, a bowling alley and a sports centre, but nothing had come of any of the plans. Now there was only a discount shop, a bookie, a post office, a bakery and a newsagent. All the other shops were boarded-up or had their security shutters permanently locked. The re-fitting of two adjoining empty premises was quite a novelty.

'Here's Bash now,' said Kev.

Bashir was striding along beside his dad, a tall man with the same deep-set eyes and high-domed forehead as his son.

'Hi,' said Bashir. 'What do you think of it?' He was pointing at number seventeen.

'It's a shop,' said Ant without enthusiasm. 'Like the one next door.' He just wanted to see this possible new recruit to the Diamonds.

'An empty shop,' said Ratso. 'So what's the big deal?'

'Yes,' said Jamie. 'What did we have to meet here for?'

'It's *our* shop,' said Bashir.

'Yours!'

Mr Gulaid started talking to one of the workmen.

'That's right,' said Bashir. 'See.'

The other workman was fixing a sign over the shop window. *Diamond Mini Mart – Proprietor Mr H Gulaid.*

'Where'd your dad get the money for a shop from?' asked Ratso. 'I thought you were always skint.'

'The family lent us some money,' Bashir explained.

'What sort of a shop is it?' asked Jamie.

'A general store,' said Bashir.

'Oh, selling generals, are you?' quipped Ratso.

Bashir ignored him. 'Do you want to see inside?'

The boys poked their heads through the door.

'Mm,' said Kev. 'Nice empty building.' It wouldn't have been cool to sound impressed.

'It will look different when it's finished,' said Bashir.

'I should hope so,' said Ratso. 'Unless you're planning to sell sawdust.'

'When does it open?' asked Jamie.

'Two weeks,' said Bashir.

Kev glanced dubiously at the empty shell of the shop. 'Think it'll be ready?' he asked.

'It will be ready,' said Bashir simply.

'So are we going to see this lad play, or what?' demanded Ant. He obviously found the Gulaids' new shop less than exciting.

'Come on,' said Kev. 'Let's make a move before Ant does my head in. You know what?' he added as they sauntered along the Parade.

'What?'

'Ant's sounding more like John every day.'

'Get lost,' said Ant. 'I don't moan.'

'You've done nothing but,' said Jamie.

Ant turned to Bashir for support. 'I ask you,' he began, 'do I moan?'

He never got his answer. At that moment a familiar bass beat filled the Parade. Kev in particular recognized the car stereo system. It was Lee Ramage's BMW, and he knew who would be at the wheel.

'Here's your dad, Guv,' said Jamie.

Kev nodded but he made no move to greet him.

'Aren't you even going to say hello?' asked Ratso.

Kev shrugged his shoulders. There didn't seem much point. It was the first sighting of Dad in weeks. He wasn't exactly Mr Family Man.

'Aren't you bothered?' asked Jamie as Kev walked on.

Bothered, thought Kev, of course I'm bothered. He'd been bothered more years than he could remember. Bothered about a man who was always just the wrong side of the law. Bothered about a man who could walk out on his family for nearly four years. Bothered about a man he loved till it hurt.

'Come on,' said Kev affecting indifference. 'Let's take a look at this striker of Ratso's.'

And that would have been it, if raised voices hadn't drawn the boys' attention back to number seventeen, South Parade.

'What's going on?' asked Jamie.

Bashir was the last to look back. 'That's our shop!'

A heated exchange had begun on the pavement outside the Mini Mart. Lee Ramage was involved in a nose to nose confrontation with Bashir's dad.

'I have every right to open a shop here,' said Mr Gulaid. 'I have all the documents. Everything is in order.'

'What about my business?' asked Lee Ramage, pointing to the other premises being renovated. 'We don't need another Paki shop. Especially not right next to mine.'

Bashir's dad met Ramage's eyes. 'You are an ignorant man,' he said. 'I am not a *Paki*. I am a Somali. And even if I were from Pakistan I would resent that word.'

Kev admired Mr Gulaid's sense of pride, but he wasn't too sure about his instinct for survival. If you've lived in the sewer as long as Lee Ramage, you come up acting like a rat.

'I'll call you what I like,' said Ramage, his contempt for Mr Gulaid ice-cold and threatening. 'I'm telling you that you can't open your shop here. Not next door to mine.'

Jamie and Kev exchanged glances. They thought they knew what Lee Ramage's business was, and it wasn't a shop on South Parade.

'And why can't I open here?' asked Mr Gulaid. 'We own different businesses. We're not in competition.'

'You keep your nose out of my affairs,' snapped Ramage. 'I'm telling you I don't want your shop anywhere near my premises.'

Kev listened to the argument then glanced at the lean, leather-jacketed man leaning on Ramage's BMW. Dad.

'You fellers,' Ramage told the bemused shopfitters. 'Out of here. Now.'

'Stay right where you are,' ordered Mr Gulaid. 'You have a job to do.'

'Now, we don't want any trouble,' said one of the shopfitters, a paunchy middle-aged man whose double chin was quivering with fright.

'That's right,' said Ramage. 'You don't. Tell him, Tony.'

Kev watched his dad remove his jacket then walk towards the three workers.

'You don't want any trouble,' he said.

As the workmen backed away, Kev's dad slammed his fist into some shelving, smashing it to bits. 'Whoops,' he said. He had a grim line in humour.

'Do your work,' Mr Gulaid told the workmen. 'These men are cheap crooks. I am going to call the police.'

Kev looked at Dad sauntering arrogantly back towards Ramage. Crooks they were. But cheap? Not when they ran half the hooky business on the Diamond.

'Now why would you want to do something silly like calling the police?' asked Ramage. 'I'm telling you that South Parade is just right the way it is. So do yourself a favour. Shut up shop and go home. That's a good boy.'

'I am not a boy,' said Mr Gulaid angrily. 'And I am not going to shut my shop.'

'Oh, you are,' said Ramage, walking slowly towards his car. 'Believe me, you are.'

Tony McGovern was about to slide into the driver's seat when he noticed Kev.

'Hello, son,' he said. 'What are you doing here?'

Kev's eyes flashed. 'I could ask you the same question.'

'Business, son.'

Kev sensed Bashir watching him, wondering which way he was going to jump. It was an uncomfortable feeling. He knew he had to take sides.

'It's the wrong sort of business, Dad.'

From his back pocket Dad pulled a roll of ten pound notes. 'There's no such thing as bad business, Kev,' he said. He peeled off a couple of notes. Kev recognized the gesture, the Lord Bountiful act. 'Here, tell your mum to buy something for you and Gareth.'

Kev backed away. 'I don't want it.'

Dad looked at the money for a moment or two then put it away. 'Suit yourself, Kev. I'll see you soon.'

Kev was aware that Bashir and the others were still watching. 'Sorry about that.'

'It's not your fault,' said Bashir.

Kev bit his lip. That's not how he felt.

'Are you all right?' Bashir asked his father.

'Yes,' said Mr Gulaid. 'I have lived through civil war. I have seen such men before, but then they had automatic weapons. Fists don't scare me. I am not frightened so easily.'

Good speech, thought Kev, but when push comes to shove you'll be singing a different tune.

'You might like to think again on that,' said the shopfitters' foreman. 'Those two have got a reputation. We're out of here.'

'But you have a job to do,' said Mr Gulaid.

'Don't you know who those two are?' asked the shopfitter. 'Because I know what they're capable of. Do yourself a favour and get out while the going's good.' He glanced meaningfully at Bashir. 'You've got a family. You don't need the aggravation.'

'You have a job to do,' Mr Gulaid repeated stubbornly.

'Not any more we don't.'

As the workmen drove off, Mr Gulaid picked up the broken shelving. 'Go and play with your friends, Bashir.'

'I don't want to go,' said Bashir. 'What if those men come back?'

Kev shuddered. *Those men.*

'I am not afraid of thugs. I have a shop to make ready.'

'You can't do it,' said Bashir. 'You don't know how.'

'Then I will find a way. Now go with your friends and let me work.'

Bashir retreated a few steps then stopped. 'I'm sorry,' he told his friends. 'I'm not coming to the rec. My dad needs me.'

He wasn't alone in being shaken by what he'd seen.

'Suddenly I don't feel much like watching football,' said Ratso.

'Me neither,' said Jamie.

'No,' said Kev, uncharacterically listless. 'I think we'll knock it on the head.'

Ant for one had still been hopeful of taking a look at Ratso's wonder player, but once even Guv had cooled on the idea, he too gave in. 'Tomorrow maybe?'

'Yes,' said Kev without a spark of enthusiasm. 'Tomorrow.'

'Your old feller's determined, isn't he?' Jamie said to Bashir as the boys sat on a crumbling wall at the end of the Parade. 'It doesn't look like he'll let it go.'

Kev stared ahead. Neither would Ramage and Dad.

Three

Wonderful, Dad. Absolutely pigging great. You stay out of my life for weeks, then just when I wonder if you've done another runner, back you come turning everything upside down. I'm not stupid, I know what you get up to. I've seen the gear stashed in Ramage's lock-up. I've seen the gangs of lads waiting on the street corner. No-hope divvies who want to get off their heads for a few hours. But why do you have to do it here, right in my own back yard? Why pick on the family of one of my best mates?

You know what, I can't look Bashir in the eye since you turned up at the Parade. I suppose I did my best to stand up to you. Yes, I did. Sort of. At least I said what you were doing was wrong. But I've got this feeling I owe Bash a heck of a lot more. He's scared to death his dad's getting himself into big trouble. He'd dead worried. Who wouldn't be? They took enough of this hassle when they moved on to the Diamond, but that was because they were different, outsiders. They were refugees and they were black.

I've got a funny feeling there's more to it this time. I mean, what's Lee Ramage so hot under the collar about, anyway? It can't be a food store. That's hardly going to do any harm to a taxi firm. I know Lee Ramage and I know what matters to him. There's only one thing that gets him angry the way he was on the Parade and that's not the colour of a man's skin, and it's not a grocery store, it's the colour of money. I don't care what he says, it's not the fact that it's the Gulaids are opening up that's bothering him, it's that they're opening up next door. He doesn't want them seeing what he's getting up to. Ramage has got something going on and I'm going to find out what it is. It'd be easier if my own dad didn't work for him. It was bad enough when he was away all those years. But not half as bad as having him round behaving the way he is. It's like my heart's an onion and he's peeling it away layer by layer.

Every time I think I'm finally in control of my life, he starts all over again, peeling away at me, killing me slowly.

What is it with me? On Sunday I was actually happy. Maybe that's what I did wrong. I dared to be happy. Well, you've punished me for that, haven't you, Dad? Maybe that's the secret. If you don't hope for anything, you can't be disappointed.

Four

John had spent a restless night hoping against hope that Carl wouldn't show. It was fine talking tough about their duel. Carrying it through was something else. John knew he had the skill and the strength to beat Carl. Any day of the week. What he didn't have was Carl's leather-thick skin, his limpet-like determination to come through.

It was something Guv had always despised about John. He was always going on about it. *When it comes to the crunch, O'Hara, you always seem to throw your hand in. When you go head to head with an opponent,* Guv would say, *you can't afford to think about anyone else, you don't care what anybody thinks of you. You just clear your mind of everything but the lad who's between you and the ball. If you let your mind get cluttered, you've had it. Focus on one thing and one thing only. Then win.*

Easy for you to say, Guv, thought John. But I'm not like you. You see a wall of flame and you imagine the buzz when you get to the other side. I just wonder how much it's going to hurt. That doesn't do me any good, though, does it? It just gets me laughed at. Well, I don't want to be laughed at. I *won't* be laughed at.

'Still here, John?' asked Dad as he lurched bleary-eyed from the bathroom. He was recovering from a lads' night out at the Lakeland, the village's pub. He'd spent the evening with a crowd from Motherwell. Apparently he'd bumped into them in the gym and they'd all become big mates. 'I thought you'd be on your way to the astro turf.'

'I don't know whether to bother,' said John. 'It's my ankle. It's still a bit stiff.'

'So we're both suffering,' said Dad. 'Pity, though. Young Carl will be disappointed.'

'When did you see *him*?' John asked abruptly. The very name of Carl Bain raised the old suspicions.

'Last night,' said Dad.

'I thought you were at the Lakeland.'

'Quite the young detective, aren't you?' said Dad with an evasive chuckle. 'No, this was earlier on. I bumped into him and his mum at the food hall. He tells me you've got a bit of a competition going.'

'Competition? Is that what he calls it?'

'Yes, he told me he was one-up. Reckons that ankle of yours is just an excuse. Told me you'd bottled out.'

John stiffened. 'He said that, did he – bottled out?

Cheeky beggar. He's a liar, a stupid, stinking liar. He never got anywhere near me yesterday.'

He jumped off the settee and pulled on his Everton away shirt. 'One-up, is he? We'll see about that. I'll show him who's bottled out.'

As he searched for his new Reeboks, John saw Dad's amused expression and realized he'd been had. He didn't really care. Dad's words had been just what was needed to get him off his backside and ready to rumble. Carl needed teaching a lesson and he was the one to do it.

'Anyone seen the sun block?' came Mum's voice from the bedroom.

'Never use it,' shouted Dad. 'I only have to look at the sun and I go a deep, natural brown.'

He was teasing. Mum had very pale, freckled skin and after a few minutes in the summer sun she looked for all the world like a boiled lobster.

'John?'

'You're joking, aren't you?' called John from the doorway. 'I can't stand the feel of it. It's dead greasy.'

'Well, I put it right here and it's gone.'

As John cycled away he could still hear her complaining that somebody kept moving her things. He had a feeling it was more of a general grumble about something, but at least it was better than screaming and shouting the way they did back home.

Three days into the holiday and it was looking good – despite the presence of the Bains. Mum and Dad seemed to be doing OK.

'Hello there, Scouse,' called Colin as John padlocked his bike. 'Where's your mate?'

'Carl? Still in bed, I hope. Better still, half-way home.'

'No love lost betweend the two of you, is there?'

John smiled grimly. 'Not a lot.'

'What's the beef?'

'He's always on my back.'

'A wind-up merchant, is he?' asked Colin. 'You know the daftest thing anybody ever said: *Sticks and stones can break your bones, but words will never hurt you.* I could always take a few knocks. It's the verbal that got to me, too.'

'Really?' said John, looking at the fit, sun-tanned instructor. 'You got skitted?'

'Of course I did. Rites of passage, lad.'

'Pardon?'

Colin gave a throaty laugh. 'Growing up, it's a bit like running the gauntlet.'

'Oh yes,' said John, catching his drift. 'I know what you mean.'

'Anyway,' said Colin, 'talk of the devil. Here he is now.'

John shielded his eyes against the strong sunlight. It was Carl, all right, walking with his affected scally swagger.

'You pathetic dweeb,' said John under his breath.

'Ready for action?' asked Carl, meeting his eyes.

'You'll see,' said John.

'Your ankle not bothering you, then?'

John was aware of the stiffness in his right leg. It hadn't just been an excuse. 'I'll be OK,' he said. 'Fit enough to bury you.'

Carl chuckled derisively. 'Didn't last the pace yesterday, did you?'

John felt a rush of indignation. He was about to answer back when Looney Toons and the rest of the boys started arriving.

'Anybody new this morning?' asked Colin, his eyes alighting on the hard core who were there every day.

A freckly, red-haired boy in a Leeds United strip raised his hand nervously.

'Right, Yorkie,' said Colin. 'Here's what we'll do first.'

It was when Carl tapped John's tender ankle and put him out of the dribble and tackle eliminator game that he realized he had a fight on his hands. Maybe it would have been better to skip coaching after all.

'What's up, O'Hara?' sneered Carl. 'Can't stand the heat?'

With his leg stiffening up with every step, John found the second game a killer. It was a new one Colin had added, a dribbling race between a line of cones. With his reduced mobility, John hobbled in a poor second behind Carl.

'Not got it today, have you, O'Hara?'

'There are still two games left,' said John irritably.

'Come on, lads,' said Colin. 'It's a hot day. Five minutes break for a drink.'

He led them to a bucket of water.

'What, no Coke?' asked Looney Toons.

'You don't want all that fizz inside you,' said Colin.

'There's ice in it,' said Yorkie, eagerly crunching a cube between his teeth.

'OK,' said Colin, laying out the cones for the next game.

John recognized it. It was the one where you ran for the bases then on to the ball, took it forward and went for goal. Under normal conditions it would be testing. With his gammy ankle it was going to be impossible.

'Ready to give up, O'Hara?' asked Carl.

'Ready to get a fat lip?' retorted John.

Suddenly he could hear Guv talking to him. *Empty your mind. No distractions. Focus.* Seizing the opportunity presented by the pail of chilled water, John stuffed a handful of ice cubes inside his right stocking. He saw Yorkie looking at him quizzically.

'Well, if the professionals wear ice-packs,' John told him, 'it's worth a go, isn't it?'

Each time John turned at the cones the nagging ache in his ankle became a fierce, stabbing pain, but he didn't pull up. The ball was waiting for him, his Holy Grail, and nothing was going to stop him getting to it first. Leaving Carl panting in his wake he took the ball in his stride and slid it gleefully under Looney Toons' body.

'I think I'm back in the race,' he told Carl.

Carl was doubled up.

John shook his head. 'You've been on that subs' bench too long,' he said. 'You're out of condition.'

'Get stuffed!'

John was up and running but he had to be on the winning side in the six-a-side game which always closed the session. When Looney Toons was picked for the opposing team he knew it would be an uphill battle.

'Hard luck, O'Hara,' said Carl. 'Looks like it's in the bag.'

Two minutes into the game Carl had even more to smile about. Looney Toons used his strength to intimidate the younger boys and had set up two goals.

'We've got to close him down,' said John.

Yorkie was the only one listening. The other boys had given up already.

'Oh, come on, lads,' said John, 'make an effort.'

But when Looney Toons got the ball again he was able to waltz past John's team-mates. There was only one thing for it. Ankle or no ankle, he had to lead by example. Focus, John lad, he told himself, will it to happen. Seeing Looney Toons squaring up for a pass to Carl, John nipped in and punted the ball forward. He could do it. He could actually do it. No backing off, no throwing his hand in, he was doing a McGovern. To his surprise and delight, Yorkie was on the end of it, trapping it neatly and side-footing it home.

Two-one down.

'Nice one, Yorkie,' said John.

'Hang on,' said Yorkie, 'here they come again.'

This time Carl had the ball.

'He's mine,' said John.

He was so full of determination, he would have tackled Godzilla in this mood. Ignoring the nagging pain in his ankle, he went in strongly on Carl and laid the ball off to Yorkie. Seeing a dark-haired boy in a Hibs shirt making space on the right, Yorkie flicked it into his path. A hard, driving shot and it was two-all. John saw Looney Toons standing red-faced with his hands on his hips.

'He's run himself out,' he told Yorkie. 'And our lads have picked themselves up. We're going to win this.'

In the event they ran away with the game seven-three.

'You know what?' said Yorkie. 'You'd make a a good club captain.'

'Thanks,' said John, then thinking of Guv, 'There's somebody back home who'd find that quite funny.'

That's when he saw a dejected Carl trying to slip away unnoticed.

'Good try,' John called, 'but not good enough.'

'Call it a draw so far,' said Carl. 'Decider tomorrow.'

'Suits me,' said John. 'Last man standing.'

Once Carl had gone, John was at last able to take a look at his ankle. As he rolled down his stocking he winced. It was red and swollen.

'Ugh,' said Yorkie. 'That doesn't half look angry. Last man standing, did you say? You'll be lucky to do any standing at all on that leg.'

Five

'Well, look who it isn't?'

Kev's flesh crept. Costello. He was propping up the Give Way sign at the top of Owen Avenue.

'Long time no see, McGovern. You haven't been hiding from us, have you?'

Kev clocked the opposition. Costello, Brain Damage, Jelly Wobble, Tez Cronin and this spotty Fifth Year whose name he'd forgotten.

'Hide from you?' said Kev, reassured by the presence of Jamie, Ratso, and Ant. 'Don't flatter yourself.'

'Hey, Gooly,' said Brain Damage, twirling a dog chain threateningly, 'I hear you and your old feller have been getting up our Lee's nose.'

Bashir bridled. He hated the nickname *Gooly*. Almost as much as he hated Brain Damage's menacing behaviour and Costello's snide grin.

'Seems you've been going where you're not wanted.'

'Not wanted by who?' retorted Kev. 'They've got a lease fair and square. You're the only ones who seem bothered.'

'That right?' sneered Costello. 'So how come your old man's rearranging furniture with his fist?'

'Leave my dad out of it!' roared Kev. Shame was a rash burning his skin.

Jamie gave him a warning look. He was losing it.

Taking a deep breath, Kev steadied himself and shrugged off the gang's attention. 'Come on, lads,' he said, 'we've better things to do than argue with these scumbags.'

'Aw, Kev baby,' chuckled Costello, 'you'll hurt our feelings.'

'I'll hurt more than your feelings,' Ant replied heatedly. He hated the thought that the gang were getting one over on them.

'Leave it,' said Kev, 'we've got to see a boy about a Championship.'

They were twenty yards up the road when Costello yelled his parting shot. 'I wouldn't bet on that Championship, McGovern,' he shouted. 'We're getting a team up ourselves.'

'You!' said Kev. 'Blessed Hearts wouldn't touch you again. Not after the way you played for them against us.'

The reminder of their two-one end-of-season reverse at the hands of the Diamonds didn't faze Costello. 'Who said anything about Blessed Hearts? There's a new outfit.'

'It's just a wind-up,' said Jamie.

'Yes,' said Ratso. 'Where'd they get the backing? Manager, strip, all that?'

'Wouldn't you like to know?' said Brain Damage. 'Wouldn't you just?'

'No way,' said Ant. 'Costello's lying through his teeth.'

'Don't be so sure,' said Kev. 'He isn't in the habit of making empty threats.'

'Anyway,' said Ant, 'are we going to take a look at this lad, or what? We've already put it off once.'

'Yes,' said Jamie. 'Let's go. Are we calling for Gord?'

'No point,' said Ratso. 'His dad's grounded him.'

'What for?'

'Nothing much. He came round ours without telling his mum. You know what his parents are like.'

Didn't they just. Bobby Jones used to manage the Diamonds once. That's how they'd ended up at the bottom of the table the previous October. It had been like being led by a lobotomized donkey.

'Poor Gord,' said Jamie.

'Poor Gord nothing,' said Ant. 'They're off to Disney, aren't they?'

Ratso nodded. 'Yes, they fly out this Friday.'

'So he'll miss the junior league final?' said Guv, wrinkling his nose in distaste. Disloyalty made him sick, and missing the big match was about as disloyal as you could get.

'Oh, come off it, Guv,' laughed Ant. 'Wouldn't you? For two weeks in America?'

'No way.'

The others stared at him in disbelief. The scary thing was, he was telling the truth.

Ratso still didn't get the joke.

'Gets everywhere, this player of yours, doesn't he, Ratso?'

'That's right,' said Ratso irritably. 'Have you seen how much space he's covered?'

'Oh, acres,' chortled Ant.

'Nah,' said Jamie. 'Miles.'

'Moves so fast,' said Kev. 'I almost think I'm seeing double.'

After the run-in with the gang, the boys wanted a laugh and Ratso was giving them the perfect opportunity.

'What is it with you lot?' demanded Ratso. 'He's good.'

'He should be,' said Jamie, finally putting Ratso out of his misery. 'There's two of him.'

'Come again?'

'Your star player,' Kev explained. 'He's *two* star players.'

Ratso watched the dark-haired boy in his blue and red Barcelona kit racing after the ball. Looking up, he crossed it perfectly – to himself!

'Neat trick, eh, Ratso?'

Still refusing to believe the evidence of his own eyes, Ratso examined the boys' shirts. Sure enough, one read number seven and the other number eleven.

'Twin brothers!' gasped Ratso.

'*Identical* twin brothers,' said Jamie.

Ratso shrugged. 'I'm a bit of a divvy, aren't I?' he asked.

'A *bit* of a divvy!' exclaimed Jamie. 'I'd say this made you the ultra-wallified, mega-plonker Space Commander of all time.'

'Except ...' said Kev.

'Yes?'

'Except the boy done good.'

'Come again?'

Ratso in particular was all ears. Just how had he done good?

'It's not one good player he's discovered,' said Kev, watching admiringly as number seven outpaced his red-faced marker yet again. 'It's two.'

Ant pondered this for a moment then slapped Ratso

heartily between the shoulder blades, a congratulation that nearly crushed the ribs of the Diamonds' skinniest player. 'Way to go, Ratso!'

Six

John stood at the front window of the cabin and watched the light fading between the pine trees. Suddenly, his chances of settling his scores with Carl were fading even more quickly.

Mum brushed back her fine, dark blonde hair. 'Over my dead body,' she said.

'But Mum,' said John. 'I've got to. It's a duel.'

'I couldn't care less if it's World War Three,' she snapped. 'You are not playing football on that leg. You should be seeing a doctor, never mind kicking a ball about.'

Mother and son were silhouetted against the blazing sunset.

'But Carl will think he's won.'

'Let him think what he likes,' said Mum. 'He'll win anyway now. You can hardly walk, let alone run on it.'

'Oh Mum, this is dead important.'

'Why?' she asked. 'Why is it so important?'

John realized he was walking on thin ice. He couldn't talk to her about Carl and the things he'd been saying. No more than he could talk to Dad about Maggot.

'I told you,' he replied doggedly. 'It's a duel. We made a pact: last man standing.'

'Then Carl's definitely won,' said Mum, 'because you can barely even get up. Don't you understand?' She applied a slight pressure to John's swollen ankle, making him gasp. 'When you feel pain like that your body is telling you to take it easy.'

'Guv would carry on,' protested John.

'Guv?'

'Kev, the captain.'

'Oh,' said Mum. 'Him.'

John realized his error in mentioning Kev. Among the parents of the Diamond players, Kev was about as popular as amputation without anaesthetic. Number one, he liked to walk on the wild side. Number two, he was Tony McGovern's son, and that was the clincher.

'But I can't just give in,' he cried. 'That's what I always do.'

Mum fixed him with a questioning look.

'I'm a wimp,' John explained. 'That's what kids say. Like when we go one-down. I can never see us getting back into the game. Guv ...'

That disapproving frown crossed Mum's face again.

'Guv says I need my backbone starching.'

'Well, I say you're selling yourself short,' said Mum.

'But it's true,' said John. 'It's always been like that. I'm always too busy looking over my shoulder, worrying about ...'

He stopped. Him and his big mouth. Some cans of worms were best left unopened.

'Worrying about what?'

Panic gripped him.

'Nothing.'

'No,' said Mum. 'Come on, Magnus Magnusson, you've started. Now you can finish.'

'Forget it.'

'John O'Hara! Either you spit it out or I'll ground you until you do – holiday or no holiday.'

John stared at his feet.

'Worrying about what?'

John was searching for something to say – anything. Anything but the truth, that is. What was wrong with him? Just when Mum and Dad seemed to be muddling through OK, he had to go and open his big mouth. The stomach cramps had begun again.

'Worrying about you,' he mumbled, finally resigned to explaining himself. 'You and Dad.'

Mum leaned forward. 'Meaning what?'

'Oh Mum, don't. Don't make me say this.'

'Meaning *what*?'

John surrendered. Taking care not to return her gaze, he chose his words as carefully as he could. Which was hard when his drumming heart seemed almost to drown his thoughts. 'I never know if you'll still be together when I get home.'

'Oh.'

As her voice faded sadly into the twilit room Mum slumped back in her seat. Her anger had evaporated. She wasn't scary any more. Suddenly she seemed to be on the verge of tears. John realized that the peace of the last few days was pitifully fragile. Blurting out his worries like that had shown just how fragile.

'We never meant to hurt you,' she said. 'You or Sarah.'

'I know,' said John, keen to make amends for raking up the past.

But Mum wasn't listening. Instead, she ran on in a hushed monotone, as if speaking to herself. 'We seem to have the knack of making one another unhappy,' she said.

John looked up at the front window. No sign of Dad yet, thank goodness.

'Always have had. I know you must find it hard to

understand, but it isn't like the films. The world doesn't end when you get married. There's something after the Happily Ever After.'

'I know, Mum,' said John. He'd let the demons out of the box and there was no returning them. He had to put a stop to this. Where did Mum think she was, confession? He didn't want to hear it, any of it.

'But whatever we've done to each other,' she continued, oblivious of his attempts to silence her, 'we really are trying to make a go of it. For your sake, yours and Sarah's. You do believe that, don't you, John?'

Another worried glance out of the window. If Dad appeared it would be a complete disaster.

'Of course I do, Mum.'

'You have enjoyed yourself, haven't you?' she continued, leaning forward. 'We wanted this holiday to be special.'

'Of course I have,' he reassured her. 'It's been boss.'

'Despite our stupid, selfish behaviour?'

'You've not stupid,' said John. 'Or selfish. Just ...'

'Just what?'

The words failed him. He shrugged forlornly.

'You can say it,' she said quietly. 'I won't mind.'

'You just don't seem to know what you want,' he said, aching with every painful word. 'One minute everything's hunky dory, the next ...'

Mum waited.

'This new start,' said John, hardly daring ask. 'It is going to work, isn't it?' Despite all the wishing, all the hoping, he suddenly realized it wasn't going to be easy. His stomach told him as much.

'I understand what you're asking,' Mum sighed. 'But I'm not sure. I hope so.'

Mum took his hands and that's the way they were sitting when Dad showed up.

'What's this?' he said. 'Sitting in the dark?'

Even in the gathering dusk, John could tell his face was flushed. Dad looked happy.

'It's a wonder you can see at all.'

It was with a tremor of surprise that John realized Dad was right. It was almost pitch black.

'Something wrong?' Dad asked.

The broad smile he'd been wearing as he opened the door was beginning to fade. When he switched on the light and saw Mum's face it vanished altogether.

'No,' said Mum, brushing away a tear with her fingers. 'Nothing wrong.'

But all three of them knew that was wishful thinking.

Seven

Summer. Don't you just hate it? These dog days are hard enough at the best of times. I watch other kids going off on holiday or for days out and I'm dead jealous. Mum can hardly afford the bus fare into town. All I'm left with is kicking my heels on the estate. Sometimes I even have to take our Gareth out with me so Mum can have a break! I get so desperate for a mention of football I hang round the radio listening for transfer news. Sometimes it gets so bad I even scan the Australian pools for the tiniest mention of the beautiful game. So it's a good job I've something to report. A bit of activity on the team-building front.

First the good news, those brothers want to join the Diamonds. Liam and Conor, they're called. I can't remember their surnames. Maybe I never even asked.

Small talk's never been my style. Plus I was keen to sell the team to them. Anyway, Ronnie will sort out the details when he signs them up. I've already been on his case about it.

Then there's the bad news. They're going away for a fortnight in Spain. Guess when? Right at the start of the season when we need them most. They'll miss both our opening games. So they're not going to be the answer to our prayers I was hoping for. It looks like I'm back to Plan A. Me in attack and John as midfield dynamo. Midfield dynamo: who am I kidding? John is to inspiration what the Lada is to high performance sports cars. But I haven't got any choice. I've started to realize that our success in the Cup was built on pretty weak foundations. I mean, we did the business with the minimum of resources and the maximum of blood, sweat and tears. We'll have to do better to challenge for the Championship. Now we've lost Dave Lafferty we don't look half as impressive. It could be that we'll even start the season relying on the services of Mattie and Carl, and that's a grim thought.

So I'd better not upset them until Conor and Liam get back off holiday. Funny how things turn out, isn't it? Less than a fortnight ago we'd won a trophy and I was convinced nobody could stay with us in the league next season. Now we're scrabbling round to find a full squad for the new season and the balance seems all wrong. The same old doubt keeps coming back to haunt me. If it is John I'm going to rely on, can he hack it? Or am I putting all my eggs in a hopeless basket.

Eight

Breakfast next morning was strained. Mum and Dad both fussed over John the way they always did when he was ill.

'How's the leg, son?' asked Dad.

'It really would be silly to go to your soccer session,' said Mum. 'It would only make it worse.'

John fixed his eyes determinedly on the television. He was the one who'd made it worse, him and his big mouth. He'd heard them talking long after he'd gone to bed. Talking, thank goodness, not quarrelling. But it wasn't the sort of talk you heard when people were getting along. Something was going on, and he didn't dare ask what. He'd rather not know.

'Come on, John,' asked Dad. 'What's eating you?'

So much for focus and willpower, John thought. It was all a waste of time.

'It's my leg,' he said feebly.

That's it. Feed them what they want to hear. Let them think you're really bothered about what Carl will think.

'Well, your mum's right, I'm afraid,' said Dad.

John could almost feel the relief in the old man's voice. After last night they wanted him to steer away from what was happening with them. He was more than happy to oblige. What good was it harping on about all the unhappiness they'd been through?

'You can do other things,' said Mum helpfully. 'The swelling's going down.'

'But not footy?' asked John tentatively, still half-hoping he could get one over on Carl.

'No,' said Mum, 'definitely not footy.'

'The pool would be OK,' said Dad. 'It doesn't put any stress on your joints ...'

'And it's free,' Mum interrupted.

'That's right,' said Dad. 'We're getting low on money. End of the month syndrome.' To make his point he picked up his wallet and shook it. 'See, nothing in here but moths.'

John smiled. 'OK, swimming it is. Either of you coming?'

'You go ahead,' said Mum. 'I'll join you in there in half an hour. It's your Gran's birthday on Tuesday and I've got to catch the post.'

'Dad?'

Mum's eyes turned his way. She too was interested in his reply.

'Maybe later,' he said. 'I promised to meet those lads from Motherwell for a quick jar. It's the last day, after all.'

'The pub doesn't open yet,' said Mum, pursing her lips.

Sensing the tension between them, John started to feel uncomfortable.

'I'd be cutting it fine, though,' said Dad. 'I promised to be in there at half eleven.'

Mum stood up, smoothed her skirt and set about her make-up. Her silence said more than words.

'I'll be off to the baths then,' said John. He was determined to get out early and avoid Carl.

'See you later,' said Mum.

'Yes, have a good swim, lad.'

John paused by his mountain bike, then thought better of riding to the pool. The previous evening he'd caught his sore ankle on the pedal a couple of times. It was agony.

'The walk will do me good,' he told himself.

Half-way up the hill to the Village Centre he glimpsed the astro turf through the trees. 'Time for a detour,' he murmured.

Leaving the main path he cut through the bracken and headed up the gentle slope. If he cut round the Lakeland he would arrive at the back of the Centre. It was a long detour but it was worth it. The expanse of forest was the quietest part of the whole holiday complex.

Negotiating the uneven floor was uncomfortable but eventually he made it ... just in time to come face to face with Carl Bain riding in the opposite direction.

'What's this?' asked Carl, skidding to a halt. 'Bottling out again.'

'It's for real,' said John. 'Look.' He started rolling down his sports sock.

'Oh,' said Carl, 'so that's your game, is it? It's a wonder you haven't got a note off your mum.'

'But you can see the swelling!'

'I can see a spineless get who wants to bail out. Last man standing, we said. Looks like it's me.'

John glared at Carl. He wanted to kill him.

'Cut it out, you. You know I've hurt my leg. You're the one who did it, for crying out loud.'

'Save it, O'Hara. I'm too old for fairy stories.'

That was it. John had taken all he could stand. 'Get off that bike,' he said, 'and I'll show you who's bottling out.'

'Drop dead, O'Hara. You're spending too much time round McGovern. You're even starting to sound like him.'

It wouldn't be a bad thing, thought John. At least I wouldn't get walked on by pinheads like you.

'Get off the bike!'

Carl shook his head. 'I'm off. I've got footy coaching to go to. Some of us don't cop out.'

John took a kick at the bike but missed and fell clumsily to the ground. Carl roared with laughter.

'You're a joke, O'Hara. A complete ...'

He never finished the sentence. As John picked himself up he saw the reason why. A little way down the slope two figures were walking hand in hand through the bracken. Dad and Carl's mum. Neither of them had noticed their sons further up the slope.

John's heart tore inside him as he watched them.

Talking.

Smiling.

Kissing.

He found himself exchanging looks with Carl. For so long they had hated one another. Now they had something in common. The pain of betrayal.

Nine

What a difference a week makes.

The Diamonds had a great turn-out to support South Sefton in the junior league Cup semi-final. Not for the final, though. I knew Gord was going to be missing. Florida, the jammy so-and-so. But what about Mattie and Carl. What about Bashir? And where was John, for goodness' sake? I'm staking everything on him for next season. So what does he do? He lets me down, like everybody else in my life. Well, like Dad anyway.

It's all over the neighbourhood. He's been giving the Gulaids more grief over their shop. Slogans painted all over the shutters. You know, the 'Go Home' variety. It's his handiwork, all right. His and Lee Ramage's. Then he cornered Mrs Gulaid in the street. She had the younger kids with her. He had her really frightened. I've hardly been able to look Bashir in the eye. He puts a brave face on it, and he swears he doesn't hold it against me. But how can you trust someone when their dad's putting the frighteners on? I'm sure Bash expects more from me. I expect more from myself. I ought to be able to do something – anything. But what? After all, he's still my dad. How do I sort that one out?

It was almost kick-off. A last check on the missing Diamonds. Nothing. Mattie and Carl aren't that important. They've never been important to the team. I wasn't even that worried about Bash. He could have been helping with the shop. They were opening next day. Yes, that had to be it. Last minute touches. John's the one I was bothered about. He was due back from holiday on Friday, but nobody'd seen him. He promised he'd be there to cheer us on. So where was he? It's a good job there's a five week break before the new season. We've got a lot of work to do.

Ten

It was a triumph for Kev. All four Diamonds were in the starting line-up for South Sefton. Nosmo had held on to the captaincy but everybody knew that Kev was the real heart of the team. He'd proved that in his second-half performance against Aigburth. As Dave Lafferty stood over the ball waiting for the signal to kick off, it was Kev who was jogging round firing up the team. By the look on his face, Nosmo didn't like it, but he barely even bothered to protest. At the whistle, Dave knocked it back to Kev. He, in turn, laid it off to Jamie.

'That's Kev's tactics,' said Ratso approvingly. 'Use the understanding they've built up playing for the Diamonds. A triangle of good passers to keep possession.'

It was working, too. Huyton harried and pressed but they were unable to get the ball.

'Craig,' shouted Kev, seeing the Ajax striker in space.

Craig weaved and jinked, trying to stay onside. Then as the ball came over he chested it down, stroked it to Scott Geraghty midway inside the Huyton half and ran on.

'It isn't on,' shouted Kev. 'They've doubled up on him. Left side.'

But Scott wasn't listening. He booted it forward only to see Craig crowded out of it.

'Didn't you see Jamie?' Kev demanded angrily. 'He was in oceans of space.'

'You don't know everything, McGovern,' Scott retorted. 'It was worth a go.'

Kev stared after him. It was one thing having the correct tactics, it was altogether another convincing players from rival teams to play together as a unit and follow them. A few minutes later Kev relieved a spell of Huyton pressure, intercepting the ball half-way inside his own half. Kenny Mason provided an outlet on the right.

'To Dave,' shouted Kev excitedly.

Dave had run into a promising position on the edge of the penalty area. But once again the opportunity was lost.

Passing up the chance to put Dave away, Kenny touched it back to his Ajax team-mate Scott. The momentum of the attack was lost and Huyton eventually came away with it. Team loyalties were disrupting South Sefton's passing game. It was bad enough when the score stayed at nil-all. It got worse. All South Sefton's early promise was lost. They were beginning to wilt under the pressure of a strong and well-organized Huyton side.

The first goal came from a corner. Terry Frost was back-pedalling desperately to meet a high, in-swinging corner kick. As he overbalanced he glanced it with the back of his head, wrong-footing Daz. It left the Huyton striker with a simple nod-in at the back post.

'Who's supposed to be on the post?' yelled Daz.

Seeing Ged Lawrence hanging his head, Daz let rip. 'Didn't I tell you to cover the post? Didn't I?'

'Sorry,' said Ged. 'But Nosmo told me to come off the line. He said I was wasting my time.'

Daz searched for Nosmo. 'Did you move Ged?' he asked.

'Yes,' said Nosmo. 'What if I did?'

'You just cost us a goal.'

'You're the one between the sticks, Kemble. Maybe if you did your job we'd still be on level terms.'

'Don't worry about it,' said Kev, resting a hand on Daz's shoulder. 'They're settling old scores. We'll get it sorted in the interval.'

'I hope so, Guv. I flipping hope so.'

As it turned out, the Diamonds survived up to half-time still only one goal adrift. It was George Rogan from South Sefton League committee, who did the sorting out.

'Let me remind you lads what this is all about,' he

said. 'We've selected the best players from our league to represent us. We did it regardless of which team you play for. We expected you to put aside any differences and play as a unit. If you don't know what I'm getting at look at any England squad. We all know there isn't much love lost between Arsenal and Spurs, or between Liverpool and Man United, but when they pull on the three lions they put up a united front. Now ...'

He glared at the boys.

'... Who thinks we've been pulling together?'

No takers.

'I quite agree,' said George. 'Kev has been playing some good stuff in the middle of the park. Scott and Kenny, too. But do you know what happens the minute we go forward? You start playing as Diamonds or Ajax or Longmoor. You don't run for each other. You don't pass to each other. It's a shambles. You're lucky you're not three or four down.'

Daz and Nosmo exchanged glances. Kev tried to do the same with Scott, but the Ajax skipper looked away.

'Let me spell it out as simply as I can,' said George. 'You can chuck it away if you want.'

Kev saw Ronnie Mintoe nodding in agreement.

'Do you know who benefits if you do? Huyton, for a start.'

The South Sefton boys glanced across at their opponents and registered the looks of satisfaction on their faces.

'And who suffers? You do. That's right. There are scouts here from Everton and Liverpool. Well, you're not going to impress anybody with a performance like that. So it's up to you, lads. I'm giving you ten minutes to do something about it, then I'm going to ring the changes. There are plenty of lads on the bench dying for a crack at Huyton.'

'Think they'll take any notice?' asked Jamie as the players picked up their orange.

'We'll make them,' said Kev. 'Look at us, for a start.'

'How do you mean?' asked Daz.

'We're all huddled together,' Kev explained. 'All four of us play for the Diamonds. It's them we should be talking to.'

He indicated the other seven players.

'Guv's right,' said Dave. 'Come on troops. Let's circulate.'

'Do you think it'll do any good?' asked Dave as the players returned to the pitch.

'Soon find out,' said Kev.

Nobody had exactly welcomed them with open arms as they'd walked round their team-mates, but they hadn't told them to get lost either.

'We got them thinking,' said Jamie.

'Maybe,' said Daz, pulling on his gloves, 'but who's going to make *them* think?' He was pointing to a group of boys making their way across the playing field from Jacob's Lane. They were all sporting the same red shirts.

'Costello and Co,' sighed Kev. 'I might have guessed they'd show. They'll love it if the second half carries on like the first.'

'Have you seen those shirts?' asked Jamie. 'Tell me if I'm wrong, but it looks like they've got a team up for next season.'

'And have you seen who else is wearing them?' added Dave.

The shirts were emblazoned with the sponsor's

name, the Liver Bird. And bringing up the rear were none other than Carl and Mattie.

'What's all this?' Kev demanded.

'Carl and Mattie are with us now,' said Costello. 'They've transferred. They're playing for us next season.'

'Us?' said Kev. 'Who's this *us*?'

'What's the matter?' asked Brain Damage. 'Can't you read?'

'You don't mean *the* Liver Bird?' asked Kev. 'The boozer on Marston Way?'

'Got it in one,' said Tez Cronin. 'They're sponsoring us in the South Sefton league.'

The Diamonds players exchanged looks of disbelief. Competition, and from the Diamond itself of all places.

'That's right,' said Costello. 'Red House have folded. We're taking their place.'

Kev stared past Costello at Mattie and Carl. 'But what are *you* doing playing for them?' he asked. 'I thought you were Diamonds.'

Jamie gave Kev a sideways glance. Surely he didn't believe that. The pair had been on their way for months.

'You can't just walk out,' said Kev. 'Not to play for them.'

'We can,' said Carl. 'And we have.'

'But why?'

'Ask O'Hara,' said Carl.

Mattie nodded in agreement. He always backed his mate.

'Come again?'

'That's right,' said Carl. 'Ask your mate O'Hara what he's been up to. Him and his old man.'

Seeing the ref looking in their direction, the Diamonds players had to re-join the team.

'Have you got any idea what they were on about, Guv?' asked Jamie.

'Not a clue,' said Kev. 'But I'll be having a word in John's shell-like.'

The gang's arrival had been a shock to the system, but there was a worse one to come on the pitch. The South Sefton boys responded to the half-time team talk. From the re-start they were playing for each other, burying their differences. There was just one problem. It had no effect on the game.

'I thought this was supposed to bring us into the match,' panted Nosmo, after scrambling clear of the third Huyton attack in the space of a minute. 'They're all over us.'

'I know,' said Kev. 'I think we've just tweaked the tiger's tail.'

Nosmo's clearance led to a corner. The Huyton winger drifted the ball high to the back post, causing panic in the South Sefton defence. Fortunately Daz was up to it, crashing through a knot of players to punch clear.

'Not again,' gasped Terry Frost, seeing Huyton sweeping forward once more.

'Go to them,' yelled Kev. 'We're defending too deep.'

But when Nosmo rushed out, his Huyton opponent simply side-stepped the challenge and crashed the ball against the post.

'Lucky escape,' said Ged Lawrence.

'We'd better stop riding our luck,' said Kev. 'You can't rely on good fortune for long.'

Huyton proved him right almost immediately. Their

fullback moved wide on the right and flicked on to their pacy winger on the overlap. As their strikers provided a possible outlet and stretched South Sefton at the back, the winger changed the point of the attack completely, lofting it square to their unmarked captain. Turning into the oceans of space left by the South Sefton defenders, he slid the ball under Daz.

'That's it, then,' groaned Nosmo. 'We're two goals adrift.'

'Listen to that wally,' snorted Jamie, 'he sounds just like John.'

'Yes,' said Dave, 'and he's the captain.'

'Talk of the Devil,' said Jamie. 'There's O'Hara now.'

Sure enough, John had just arrived. On his own. Only his secret pain to keep him company.

'How's it going?' he called, joining Ant, Joey, Jimmy and Ratso on the touch line.

'Dire,' said Jamie. 'We're two down.'

'Is that O'Hara?' snarled Kev, jogging across. 'Where've you been?'

'I couldn't get away,' John replied defensively.

'I'll be talking to you after the game,' said Kev.

'Don't worry about Guv,' said Jamie. 'You know how he hates losing.'

Huyton soon found out just how much. Stung by Huyton's dominance he began to hustle and bustle, pressurizing the player in possession. His example was infectious. Even Nosmo started to pick himself up.

'That's the style, lads,' he bawled. 'Don't give them any time on the ball.'

Kev gave Jamie a sly smile as he jogged by. 'Telling your granny how to suck eggs,' he whispered.

'Who cares?' said Jamie, 'so long as we get back into it.'

It was a bit of sheer opportunism by Dave Lafferty that gave South Sefton their chance. Seeing the Huyton keeper dawdling over the ball he rushed him. Hustled by Dave, the goalie fluffed his clearance, driving it against the striker's chest. Seizing on the error, Dave flicked the ball on to his right peg and scored from ten yards.

'Yes!' shrieked Ratso, leading the applause. 'We're back in the game.'

Of the cluster of Diamonds players on the sidelines only John was muted in his reaction.

'Something wrong?' asked Ratso.

John nodded.

'Do you want to talk?'

John shrugged his shoulders, but it was obvious he did.

On the pitch Kev and Nosmo were beginning to turn the tide in midfield, intercepting Huyton's passes, blocking their forward balls, forcing them into errors. It was a completely different match.

'Guv, Guv,' yelled Jamie, racing out to the left flank.

Kev knocked it down the line and ran on to receive the return ball. Jamie considered it, but plumped for Kenny Mason bursting into the penalty area. Kenny's cushioned header dropped invitingly in Kev's path. There was only one idea in his head. Blast it.

Two-all.

Suddenly the divisions were opening in the Huyton ranks as they started squabbling with one another over the loose marking. A couple of substitutions steadied the ship, but South Sefton were worth their equalizer.

'Push up,' shouted Nosmo. 'We're going for the winner.'

'Hang on,' said Kev. 'Where are you going?'

'Into attack. Where else?'

'We shouldn't commit too many men forward,' warned Kev. 'It's our control of midfield that's bringing results.'

'Behave,' said Nosmo. 'We've got them rocking.'

It looked like he was right when Scott Geraghty headed against the bar and Dave missed the rebound by inches.

'You're too cautious, McGovern,' said Nosmo.

South Sefton went close again from a corner, Jamie bringing out a spectacular save from his well-struck volley. That's when Huyton caught them napping.

Seeing his forwards outnumbering the South Sefton defenders, the Huyton keeper launched it downfield. A neat flick forward and the Huyton captain was clear with only Daz to beat. Daz came out as far as the penalty spot, arms outstretched. Delaying his shot, the Huyton skipper drifted left. Daz could have dived in, but chose instead to shadow his man. When the Huyton player finally made his decision and tried to chip the keeper, Daz was able to get his fingertips to the ball and push it behind.

'Great save,' said Nosmo.

'Yeah, and one I shouldn't have had to make. You left me exposed.'

Kev nodded approvingly. As he brought the ball away from the D, the ref blew for full time.

'I feel like I've been in a game,' said Jamie.

'Yes, me too,' said Dave. 'A draw's a fair result, I suppose. At least we've stopped them getting a hat trick of wins.'

'Don't let Guv hear you say that,' said Daz. 'Where is he, anyway?'

'Over there,' Jamie told him. 'Giving John earache over arriving late.'

'So where have you been?' roared Kev. 'And what have you done to Carl? We still need him and Mattie, you know. With them and Dave gone we've only got ten players. We're in trouble, and it's all down to you.'

'Sorry, Guv,' said John. He was waiting for Kev's anger to run its course.

'Sorry's no use,' said Kev, unimpressed. 'And what's so important you can't come along and support us?'

John's eyes welled up with tears. Without another word he fled towards the road.

'Well,' said Kev, looking around. 'What was the big flaming deal?'

It was Ratso who answered. 'Not much, Guv,' he replied. 'Only that his Dad's just left home.'

Kev watched the retreating figure of John O'Hara. He suddenly felt very stupid.

Eleven

Everything seems to be coming down round my ears.

I didn't mean to do that to John. How was I to know his old feller had walked out? Before he went away he'd been full of it, talking tactics, banging on about the way playing at Jacob's Lane gave South Sefton home advantage in the tournament, and really looking forward to his holiday in the Lakes. I'm not cold-hearted. After all, I know what it means. It's just ... Oh, I don't know. I'm all out of excuses. I was fired up after the match and when I saw him turn up late like that I just snapped. Everything had been coming at me. Bashir going walkabout, Mattie and Carl going over to Costello's gang.

Then of course there's Dad getting up to his old tricks. Mum's actually talked about stopping him seeing me and Gareth. A bad influence, she calls him. Maybe, but I need him. Stupid, isn't it? All that pain and I'm still hoping against hope he'll come good and be a proper father to us. That's all I want, all I've ever wanted, to be part of a normal family. I just want two parents who love me better than anyone in the whole world.

It all got too much so I blew. Just a few minutes ago I was a hero. We'd held a much better side to a well-deserved draw and a lot of it was down to me. When I came off the pitch they were all talking about me, saying what a motivator I was. They're still talking about me, but they're not saying anything good now. I've kicked John when he was down and I've blown a hole a mile wide in the Diamonds' prospects for next season. I've got the rest of the summer break to put things right. Nothing else can go wrong, can it?

Twelve

The following Monday saw the Diamonds hanging round the top of Owen Avenue.

'I could ask my cousin,' said Dave.

'Is he any good?' asked Kev, brightening. If he was related to Dave maybe there was hope after all.

'Not really,' said Dave, 'In fact, he's got two left feet. But at least you'd start the season with eleven players. Until those brothers come back off holiday.'

'I'll keep him in mind,' said Kev. 'But we need more than a stop-gap. Surely one of you knows somebody who can play a bit.'

Blank faces greeted him.

'Think,' said Kev. 'There must be someone.'

'I can't see it,' said Ant. 'All the decent players have been snapped up by teams already. Especially now this Liver Bird lot have got together. There's even competition on the estate now.'

'So what do we do?' asked Jamie.

Ratso paused. 'There's always ... No, it's a stupid idea.'

'Go on,' said Kev. 'Spit it out.'

'You'll only shoot me down in flames,' said Ratso.

'No we won't,' said Kev.

'Yes you will.'

'Ratso,' Kev growled, 'we won't laugh at you and that's as promise. Just tell us.'

'I know where there'll be a few players in search of a team,' said Ratso. 'And I'm certain they'll still be available.'

'Then tell us,' said Kev.

'Yes,' Ant chipped in hopefully. 'Put us out of our misery.'

'Red House Rovers,' said Ratso, reluctantly biting the bullet. 'You heard Costello. The team's folded. There must be a few of them who still want to play.'

He saw everyone looking at him.

'This a joke?' asked Jimmy.

'No.'

'Then you are,' snorted Kev. 'Have you forgotten *why* they folded?' They were bottom of the league. They're rubbish.'

'They must have had some good qualities,' argued

Ratso, obviously wondering what had happened to Kev's promise to take his suggestion seriously.

'Like what?' stormed Kev, furious at having his time wasted. 'What was the score against us? Tell me that.'

'Thirteen-two,' Ratso admitted. 'But …'

'But what?' asked Jamie. 'Don't you get it? We put thirteen past them. They were rubbish.'

'They scored two,' said Ratso lamely.

'He's off his crust,' said Ant, screwing a finger into his temple.

With that, the rest of the Diamonds walked off towards South Parade, leaving Ratso standing on his own.

'Well, at least I had an idea,' called Ratso. 'That's more than any of you came up with.'

'You're a sad case, Ratso,' said Kev.

'No, I'm not,' shouted Ratso, crossly. 'I'm the one who discovered the brothers and I'm the one who's trying to repair the damage you've just done. You've always been on Carl and Mattie's backs, remember. You probably had something to do with them quitting. And you've just had a go at John. What if he clears off on us? We won't even have ten players. Go on, Guv, what makes you so rotten wonderful?'

Kev stopped in his tracks.

'You tell me my idea's stupid,' said Ratso stubbornly. 'Then come up with something better.'

There was a long pause before Kev answered. 'I can't,' he said. 'That's why we're going to give yours a shot.'

It was his turn to be stared at.

'This is a joke, right?' said Ant.

'I'm afraid not,' said Kev. 'Ratso's right. Beggars can't be choosers. The way things stand we can't even field a side. Until the brothers get back from Spain we've got a squad of ten.'

'But you said it yourself,' Jamie protested. 'Red House are useless.'

'But they're still footballers,' said Kev. 'Or at least they'd like to be. Maybe there are one or two who are half decent.'

He looked around at the doubtful faces. 'We were bottom once, remember.'

No change in the boys' expressions.

'It won't hurt to give it a go.'

Another pause.

'Well?'

'OK,' said Jamie, 'I'll go along with it.'

'Not much choice, have we?' said Jimmy. 'Uncle Ron will be able to get the lads' addresses.'

'That's it, then,' said Kev. 'We go with Ratso's idea.'

Ratso beamed. Nobody else did.

'Oh, by the way,' Kev added, 'if this all goes pear-shaped it's down to you, Ratso.'

The smile vanished.

'Only joking, Rats,' chuckled Kev, tousling Ratso's hair. 'Only joking.'

As the Diamonds turned into South Parade they were laughing like hyenas.

But what they saw next killed the laughter stone dead.

'What happened, Bash?' asked Jimmy, joining Bashir on the kerb in front of the shop.

Bashir looked instinctively at Kev. 'They came back,' he said.

'Flipping heck,' said Ant, peering through the Mini

Mart's shattered front door. 'They didn't half go to town.'

Kev's face had drained of blood. 'You're sure it was ...' He was unable to finish the sentence. His voice cracked before he could say Dad or Lee Ramage's names.

'It was the same men,' said Mr Gulaid, appearing from inside his shop. 'Who else would do such a thing?'

There was no disguising his hostility. He had always been friendly to Kev. Until now.

'They knew we were opening tomorrow,' said Bashir. 'And they knew everywhere would be quiet on Sunday afternoon. They just waited for the newsagent to close.'

'This is why you missed the match?' asked Ratso.

Bashir nodded. 'Dad and I were on our way to Jacob's Lane to watch. Dad wanted to check on the place. That's when we found it like this.'

'Can you put it right?' asked Jamie.

'What would be the point?' asked Mr Gulaid. 'They would only come back and do the same again.'

'You mean they've won?' asked Jimmy.

Mr Gulaid tossed a broken display unit on to the pavement. 'Yes.'

'But that's rotten,' said Ant.

Nobody was arguing, least of all Kev.

'I'm sorry, Bash,' he murmured.

Everybody turned towards him.

'I'm sorry, I'm so sorry.'

They were shocked to see something you didn't expect from Kev McGovern. There were tears in his eyes.

PART THREE

Showing Promise

One

Ever felt like you were talking to yourself?

That's how it was with John today. It's taken me three whole weeks to get him to talk to me. OK, scrub that. It's taken three whole weeks for Jimmy, Ant and Jamie to get John to talk to me. I can't say I blame him for being stand-offish. I virtually accused him of wrecking the team. Then, to top it all, I trampled all over his feelings. He's as bruised as a windfall apple, that lad. The trouble is, he won't talk. I know, I know. I'm not the cry-on-the-shoulder type, but I know what it's like for him. We've heard that his parents have split up, but that's about it. He just clams up about the rest.

Anyway, he agreed to meet me down the rec. Our conversation was more like a yes, no interlude.

Me: Sorry about the way I spoke to you.

Him: You should be.

Me: I am. Honest. Do you forgive me?

Him: Why should I?

Me (wishing I could crawl away and die): Because we need you.

Him: Go on.

Me: I've got plans for you.

Him: Yes?

Me: You do still want to play for us, don't you?

Him: Yes.

Me: Midfield suit you, alongside Ratso?

Him: Yes.

Me: Don't you want to know where I'll be playing?

Him: No.

And that's about it. I asked, he answered. It was hard work, I can tell you, and I came away wondering what was going on in his head. It was like fighting smoke. I just couldn't make contact. The only thing I did come away with was his intention to carry on playing for the Diamonds. I just wish that made me feel better, but it doesn't. He didn't sound like he was ready to set the world on fire.

It just gets worse. Not only have I stepped on John's toes, there's the Bashir thing, too. Dad won't admit to it, but I'm sure it was him and Ramage who turned the shop over. It just lies there, empty and full of broken units. Bashir's dad hasn't given up the lease yet, but he hasn't made any move to fit it out again. Meanwhile, Lee Ramage's place next door is taking shape. Brain Damage and Costello are always hanging round there now, taunting us. What makes it worse is Mattie and Carl are really well in with them. The whole lot of them patrol the estate in their new red shirts. They've thrown down the gauntlet and we're in no condition to pick it up.

I'm running on empty, I can tell you.

Two

John spotted the suitcase the moment he came through the door. A skip in his chest as his hopes rose.

'Dad?'

'It's not what you think,' said Sarah, intercepting him in the hall. 'He isn't coming back.'

'What then?'

A short pause, then the simple truth. 'He's come to pick up the rest of his things.'

A jolt in the pit of his stomach as his hopes sank. 'But where's he been?'

As if in answer to John's question, Dad appeared at the living room door. He looked drawn and somehow out of place in his own home. It wasn't the return John had been aching for. Dad wasn't staying.

'Where've you been?' There was accusation in John's voice. They'd had one brief phone call since Dad walked out.

'I stayed at a friend's for a few days,' Dad replied.

Sarah raised her eyes impatiently. He was being evasive and she wanted John to know it. 'You may as well tell John the truth,' she said.

Dad's shoulders sagged. He stood there for a moment like a guilty schoolboy. 'I've moved in with Sue,' he admitted in a low voice.

John frowned. Sue?

'Sue Bain,' said Sarah.

Then the gnawing sickness was gone, replaced by an anger that blazed through his veins like liquid fire.

'Carl Bain's mum!' cried John. 'You're actually living there? Already! But he's my worst enemy. You can't do this to me.'

'It's for the best, son.'

'What are you talking about?' John was beside himself. 'Can you imagine what everybody's going to be saying? They'll all be laughing at me.'

Dad scratched nervously at his stubble. 'It's better to make a clean break now,' he said. 'It will save us all a lot of pain in the long run. This,' he looked round the house, 'well, it was a mistake. Your mum and I have just been playing at marriage. We should have had the guts to call it off years ago.'

'What about us?' asked John, his voice trembling.

'Me and Sarah, were we a mistake, too?' He detested the feeble sound of his own voice. It was full of self-pity, but that wasn't all. There was the desire to hurt, and his barb hit home. Dad looked like he'd taken a punch. He was reeling from John's question.

'Don't say that, John, please don't ever say that.'

John watched the effect of his words, but he didn't feel any satisfaction.

'How do you expect him to feel?' spat Sarah. 'This isn't a family, it's a comic turn.'

John was an amateur when it came to getting back at his parents. She was a professional. With years of experience behind her, she could turn it on at will.

'Sarah!'

Mum had arrived on the scene. Her eyes were red. She'd been crying.

'Why her, Dad?' asked John, screaming inside. 'Why Mrs rotten Bain? I've got to go to school with her stupid son.'

'It just happened,' said Dad lamely.

'Nothing *just happens*,' said Sarah. 'You decided to do it.'

John stared at Dad for a moment, taking in the news, then his expression changed. 'It was no coincidence, was it? You knew she'd be at Lakeland.'

'Oh, he knew all right,' said Sarah. She'd lost patience with her parents years ago. Now she wanted their suffering to equal hers and Johns.

'You mean they planned it?' gasped John, his mind working overtime. 'Yes, Carl said they booked late. You asked her to come, didn't you? It wasn't for us, it was for her. I bet there never were any fellers from Motherwell, either. It was all a story. You were messing about all the time. You were meeting *her*.'

John looked round for confirmation of his suspicions. Mum closed her eyes and turned away, but Sarah gave him his answer. She nodded grimly.

'The whole thing,' John cried, his voice breaking, 'our holiday, the new start, all those promises, they were all lousy, stinking lies, weren't they?'

Dad reached out to comfort him. 'John ...'

John backed away. 'Weren't they, weren't they, *weren't they*?'

Dad was almost pleading with him. 'I didn't want it to be like this,' he said. 'I didn't want to hurt anyone. You don't know what it's been like ...'

Mum's eyes flashed a warning. 'Don't say it,' she said. 'Don't you dare make it any worse. Don't say another word.'

Dad's mood changed abruptly. Gone was the pathetic grovelling. He became hard and bitter. 'Fine,' he said. 'Have it your way. I was going, anyway. I don't know what game you're playing but the kids will know the truth soon enough, won't they?'

John looked at Sarah. So far she had seemed aware of everything that had been happening. This time even she looked confused.

'What are you on about?' she asked.

'Ask your mother,' snarled Dad, snatching up the suitcase. 'Don't blame me for everything. She's no angel, either. That's right, it's her turn to come clean.'

With that, he stormed out of the house.

'Mum?'

She threw up her hands. 'Leave it, Sarah. Just leave it. I think we've all said enough for one day.'

'But ...'

'*Enough!*'

Mum's shout cracked in the air. Even Sarah knew

—— 101 ——

better than to argue any further. While Mum stamped back into the living room, they retreated to the kitchen.

'This is terrible,' said John. 'Terrible.'

'I'm glad I've got this,' said Sarah. She'd picked up an envelope from the work surface.

'What is it?' asked John.

She handed him the typewritten letter.

'Read it.'

'University of East Anglia!' he exclaimed. 'You mean … ?'

'That's right, I got in as well. The letter came this morning. I'm getting a place down there with Simon. I just hope I can make a better job of things than they ever did.'

John felt numb. The hole that had been blasted in his life seemed to be opening wider all the time.

'You and Beano,' he asked, 'you're not going to get married, are you?'

Sarah threw back her head and laughed loudly. 'Marriage – who said anything about marriage? Mum and Dad haven't been very good adverts, have they? We're going to share a flat. Full stop, end of story.'

'I'm never getting married,' said John. 'Not ever. I'd die first.'

'Can't blame you,' said Sarah.

'I'm going to have a hamster instead. Maybe a few fish in a tank.'

Sarah laughed.

'Much safer.'

John smiled at her. Her humour was something to hang on to, a rock in the rapids.

'When do you leave?'

'October.'

He hung his head. Last man standing, that was him all right. 'I'll miss you,' he said.

'Whoa, don't go all soppy on me, little brother.'

'I will, though,' John insisted. 'I will miss you. You're not like them. You never make a promise you wouldn't keep.'

'You know why?' asked Sarah.

'No.'

'I never made any promises at all.' She dabbed at her eyes with a paper handkerchief. 'I've learned it's the best way.'

Three

Kev retrieved the ball from the far side of the rec and turned. Judging by the long shadows cast by the other boys, it was getting late. Jamie was the closest of his team mates.

'So what do you think, Jay?'

Jamie looked at the former Red House goalkeeper, Dougie Long. The Diamonds had spent the last hour putting him through his paces in a fast and furious five-a-side game. 'Scraping the barrel a bit, aren't we?' he whispered to save the boy embarrassment.

'Maybe,' said Kev. 'But the others were worse.'

Ant and Ratso joined them.

'What do you think?' asked Kev.

'I'm no expert,' Ant replied. 'But he doesn't seem too bad between the sticks. It looks like he just had a lousy defence in front of him.'

'I agree,' said Ratso. 'But it's an outfield player we

need. Daz is probably the best keeper in the league. No room for him there.'

Dougie was getting impatient. 'Am I in, or what?'

The rest of the Diamonds had joined the discussion by now.

'Give us a minute, Dougie,' said Kev. 'I need to talk it over with the lads.'

Dougie dropped to the ground and picked at the grass. He didn't look very hopeful.

'He'll be good cover for Daz,' said Joey.

'That's what Ratso's been saying,' said Kev. 'But it's in defence or midfield we need him. Is he good enough?'

Dougie had played the first half in goal and the second upfield.

'He's slow,' said Bashir.

'Compared to you,' said Joey, 'everybody's slow.'

'There's something else,' said Gord. 'He panics a bit when you close him down.'

'I think the Liver Bird got the pick of the Red House team when they folded,' said Ant. 'I hear three of them have signed up with the gang.'

'That's something in Dougie's favour,' said Jamie. 'He turned Costello down flat.'

'I never knew that,' said Jimmy. 'How come?'

'Simple really,' said Jamie. 'He hates his guts.'

'Now that's something else in his favour,' said Daz, clearly impressed.

'OK,' said Kev. 'Decision time, lads. Let me put it like this. On the down side, he's always been a keeper so we'll be playing him out of position. He's slow and he gives the ball away under pressure. Good points; he'll provide cover for Daz, he's got two legs and he hates Costello and Co.' He gave a broad grin. 'There are just ten days to the big kick-off, and we're still a man short. Your decision, gentlemen.'

The vote was unanimous.

'Dougie,' called Kev. 'You're in. We'll get you a registration form. Ronnie's got them round his house.'

Dougie punched the air. 'What's our first match?' he asked.

'You're going to love this,' said Kev. 'It's a baptism of fire. Tell him, Ratso.'

'Only the champions,' Ratso replied. 'Longmoor Celtic.'

'And don't go thinking they're an easy option just because some of them have gone up into the next age division,' said Jimmy. 'Uncle Ronnie says the new crop of players are just as good. Maybe even better. It's a real nursery of talent. I just found out that Nosmo King's dad played for Tranmere for three seasons. Until he broke his leg.'

'But the Longmoor game isn't half of it,' said Kev. 'The second match is the one I've got my eye on.'

Judging by the puzzled looks on the team-mates' faces, nobody had looked beyond the Longmoor game. Nobody except Ratso.

'That's right,' he said. 'It could be a bit special.'

'Why,' asked Gord. 'What's the big deal?'

'Here your starter for ten,' said Ratso, his eyes twinkling. 'It's a local derby against the league's newcomers.'

'Not the Liver Bird!' gasped Daz. 'You don't mean we've got Costello and Co that early on?'

'Oh, but we have,' said Kev. 'And those brothers we met won't be back until the following week. We've got to face them with an under-strength side. Think we can do it?'

The defiant roar that met Kev brought a smile to his face.

'Anyway,' said Ant. 'I'm off. Going my way, Dougie?'

Dougie nodded.

'Welcome to the Diamonds,' Doug,' shouted Kev.

He jogged to catch up with Jamie and Bashir. 'That was a good evening's work,' he said.

'Yes,' Jamie agreed. 'But we've still got a problem.'

Kev stared blankly.

'John,' said Bashir. 'Or had you forgotten? He was the only one missing this evening.'

Kev didn't like the tone of Bashir's voice, but he went easy on him. Bashir was still feeling sore at him over what Dad had done to the shop.

'I haven't forgotten,' said Kev. 'To tell the truth, I've been leaving him alone. I think he needs time for the dust to settle at home.'

'You know where his dad's gone, don't you?' asked Jamie.

'No, where?'

'He's only moved in with Carl Bain's mum.'

'Never!'

'It's true.'

'That's torn it,' said Kev. 'What's he going to think when he sees the fixture list?'

'That Liver Bird game, you mean?' asked Jamie.

'Of course the Liver Bird game,' said Kev. 'The stakes are getting higher all the time.'

'So what are we going to tell him?' asked Bashir.

'If he ever shows up,' said Jamie gloomily.

Kev puffed his cheeks and blew hard.

'Nothing,' he answered. 'Not a dicky bird.'

Four

It was on another sunny evening a week later that John finally returned to the Diamonds fold.

'You made it, then,' said Kev.

There was relief in his voice. He'd been standing in the car park in front of South Road community centre for nearly half an hour, willing John to show up. By the time he finally made his entrance, the knot of anxiety in Kev's stomach was the size of a football.

'What's up, Guv?' asked John, eyeing his skipper. 'Think I'd buckle under the pressure?'

Kev was slightly taken aback by John's prickliness. His face must have given him away, because John immediately added to his sharp retort.

'I suppose the lads all know what's happened by now.'

Kev glanced at the team gathering round Ronnie Mintoe for the first training session of the new season.

'Yes, they've a good idea. No need to worry, though. A lot of us have been through it.'

John nodded wryly. The Diamonds' parents had enough problems to fill a whole series of American chat shows.

'It's OK anyway,' John said as nonchalantly as he could manage. 'It's not like it came as a big surprise.'

It had, but he was too proud to admit that to Kev.

'Ready to play some football?' asked Kev.

John smiled. 'Am I ever!'

As they approached the boys clustered round Ronnie, John frowned.

'Something wrong?' asked Kev.

'Who's that?'

'Dougie. Dougie Long. He used to play for Red House.'

John nodded. 'That's how I know him. Played in goal, didn't he?'

'That's right.'

'So what's he doing here?'

'We've drafted him into the side. We were a man short. You know, what with Mattie and …' He pulled up short.

'It's all right,' said John, 'You can say his name. Carl. Finally resigned, have they?'

It was only now, listening to him, that Kev realized how little John had been in touch over the summer break. He was going to mention the news about the Liver Bird team when he thought better of it.

'Ronnie's not moving Daz, is he?'

'Don't be soft,' said Kev. 'We're playing Dougie on the right side of midfield. He lacks pace but he ought to be able to get in a few tackles. I flipping hope so. That's where you come in, keeping it solid in the middle of the park.'

'You reckon I can do it, then?'

Kev decided to keep his doubts to himself. 'Of course I do, and Ronnie agrees with me.'

By the time they joined the team Ronnie was well into his pep talk.

'We're lucky,' whispered Kev. 'We've missed the waffle.' He imitated Ronnie's voice: 'You've had your summer holidays, now it's time to roll up your sleeves and get down to work.'

Ronnie wasn't too pleased with Kev muttering at the back. 'Would you like to do this team talk, Kevin?'

'Kind of you to ask,' said Kev cheekily. 'But no thanks. I wouldn't want to put you out of a job.'

The rest of the Diamonds giggled appreciatively.

'Anyway,' said Ronnie, doing his best to ignore Kev. 'What was I saying? Oh yes, it's time to roll up your sleeves and get down to work.'

For a moment John stared at Kev wide-eyed, then they both spluttered with laughter.

The training session was mostly fitness routines: stretching, running and turning, shuttle runs, jogging round the field, and sprints. By the time they'd finished Dougie was breathing heavily.

'I never did any of this malarkey when I was playing for Red House,' he panted.

'Complaining?' asked Kev.

'No, not really.'

'Because if you were,' Kev told him bluntly, 'I'd have to remind you that you ended up bottom of the table.'

Dougie took the criticism without a word. He was making a mental note: when I'm around the Guv'nor I'd better choose my words carefully.

'Right, lads,' called Ronnie. 'Gather round. I want to keep this short so you can get off home. You all know it's Longmoor on Sunday.'

John's eyes widened. 'Some opening game,' he exclaimed.

'OK,' said a smiling Ronnie Mintoe. 'Most of you know it's Longmoor on Sunday. Don't think that just because John King, Mick Rathbone and—'

'Skinhead,' said Kev.

'Thanks,' said Ronnie, slightly miffed. 'Just because

those three are now playing for Longmoor's senior team it doesn't mean the new team aren't a good side. They've still got eight of the Championship side intact and from what I've heard on the grapevine the three new boys are all cracking players. We'll be going into the new season without Dave and that's a big loss. We've got some new blood on the way into the side, but two of our new recruits aren't available for the first two matches. That means we start the season without any subs. Not an ideal situation but we'll just have to manage. Now, tactics.'

'You talk tactics!' declared Dougie. 'We never.'

'No wonder you ended up bottom,' said Jimmy, saving Kev the bother.

'We go with the usual flat back four,' said Ronnie. 'That's Jimmy, Gord, Ant and Joey. John, Dougie and Ratso, you're the midfield trio. Up front, Bashir on the left flank and Jamie and Kev hunting through the middle. And that's about it. You've played them before so you know what to expect. They're strong and they're fast. I want you to press them all the way, harry them every time they get the ball. If we let them play we're digging our own graves. So you've got to keep it tight. See you Sunday, lads, bright and early.'

'See you Ronnie,' chorused the team.

Kev was heading for home in the company of Bashir and Jamie when he saw his Uncle Dave boarding up a broken window. Dave was a community worker at the Centre and doubled as a handy man.

'Hi, Dave,' he shouted.

'Hi there, Kev.'

The boys had reached the road when Kev came to a dead halt.

'Hang on,' he said. 'Bash, is your dad still interested in opening that shop?'

'I don't know,' said Bashir. 'He hasn't said anything about it for weeks.'

'Then ask him,' said Kev, 'because I've just had an idea.'

Five

Maybe, just maybe, I can breathe out now. That's the way I feel, like I've been holding my breath all summer in case something else went wrong. Now here I am within spitting distance of the new season and I'm starting to feel the first glimmers of hope.

John's re-surfaced at last. I was having doubts about whether he ever would. I was younger than him when my own dad walked out, but I haven't forgotten what it did to me. Mum was down at school every five minutes. The teachers just couldn't handle me. I was hurting other kids and hurting myself. That's right, I started pinching myself. Really hard, all the way down my arms. Then it was the fires. I was setting light to things all over the estate. The kid from Hell, that's what everybody called me. It went on for a couple of years off and on, until the time I set one in this pensioner's garden. He collapsed and died, right there on the spot. I never meant it to happen, sometimes I even wish it had been me instead, but since when did life take any notice of what I want?

That's how we ended up living on the Diamond. The council had to re-house us after what happened. Mum's never really been the same since. I think she's always expecting it to start all over again. It won't, though. I keep telling her that, and maybe one day she'll believe me. I'm tougher now, but more in control. That's what the Diamonds have done for me. All that rage, all that fire, I put it into the game, into turning my mates from divvies into heroes. I'm not saying John's sunk as low as I did and I'm not saying he can pick himself up in quite the same way, but the Diamonds are there for him. Through us he can begin to fight back.

In fact, the fightback's starting all round. We've pulled the team back together – just. I don't know if we can win this Sunday but at least we're in a position to try. Just a few weeks ago I wondered if we'd even be able to field a team.

Most important of all, I think I can do something to help Bashir. I don't know what's been wrong with me. I saw one of my best mates getting pushed around. So what did I do about it? Nothing. I lay down and took it, just like everybody else. Some fighter I've been. And it's worse for me to give in. I mean, it's my own dad who's causing all the aggro. Well, I've got news for you, Dad, I love you but I won't sit back and let you wreck everything.

Six

Sometimes, when you know something really, really bad is going to happen, life goes into freeze-frame. It happened to John on Saturday afternoon and it came out of the blue. He'd been happy as he walked into the house. He'd played well, even starred, in an impromptu kick-about with some of the Diamonds down the rec. Now, as he stopped dead in the hallway, it was as though all the bonds tying him to his mates began to snap one by one. What he saw made him feel so alone. It was only a carrier bag, but a strange one, for a Sports Shop in Manchester. It isn't much, an unfamiliar carrier, but it was enough to set alarm bells ringing. Who did he know who ever went to Manchester? Outside, the thunder storm that had been building all afternoon had just broken. A dull rumbling was spreading over the city and lancing rain was pounding the windows. But the clincher was a small item next to the carrier. An inlaid mahogany box with brass hinges.

'What's this?' asked John. The question wasn't directed to anybody in particular. He already knew the answer. He only knew one chess player.

John heard the living room door creaking slowly open. He didn't turn.

'I recognize this,' he announced, picking up the wooden box. A chess set: *To an excellent teacher.*

He started to swing it in his right hand, slowly at first then more quickly.

'Yes, I recognize it, all right.'

'Chess club somewhere, was it?' he asked, the resentment building in his voice. 'Is that why you brought it along? You've been having a little game of chess with our pressie.'

That's when he turned, his face set in a look of pained rage. He saw its owner standing next to his mother. His hand was resting on her shoulder, like he owned her.

'I think this is yours,' he shrieked. 'Maggot!'

As the word escaped from his lips he flung the box as hard as he could in the direction of Mum and Mr May. It hit the door jamb and burst open, spilling pieces all over the floor.

'I hate you, Maggot,' he yelled, making for the door.

'And,' he glared at Mum, 'I hate you, too. My teacher,' he screamed. 'My flaming teacher! How could you?'

Without another word he flung open the door and ran into the Close where his bike was still propped against the front gate.

'John,' shouted Mum. 'Come back inside.'

But he had no intention of going inside. He had no intention of doing anything either of his parents said. Not ever again. Jumping on his bike he pedalled furiously down the road.

'John!'

He rode head down, driving himself into the hard, stinging rain.

'You're not worth a carrot,' he yelled into the storm. 'Either of you.'

At the top of the Close he swung out on to Fairfax Avenue, narrowly missing a black Mondeo. Neither the near miss nor the loud blast from the vehicle's horn made him so much as slow down. By the time he hit the Parade he was drenched to the skin. He could actually feel the streams of water running between his shoulder blades. But still the downpour didn't relent. As he flashed past the bakery he heard somebody shouting his name.

'John?'

He glimpsed Bashir. He was standing in the doorway of the shop with Guv and his Uncle Dave. There was a girl, too. Guv's cousin Cheryl. John didn't even raise his hand to acknowledge them. Somehow he felt they would all know what had happened, and that meant they'd be laughing at him. The whole world laughs at a loser.

'John,' Guv yelled after him as he turned on to Owen Avenue. 'What's wrong?'

Stupid question, thought John. What's wrong? Everything. Every rotten lousy thing in his life. He'd done what was expected, hadn't he? He'd handled Dad walking out, stuffing the pain he felt deep down inside himself. He'd even got along to training, joining in the routines, laughing along with the jokes. He'd done what Guv always said: focus, empty your mind of everything except the problem facing you. Sounds fine, but what if every time you start to handle one problem another comes back to hit you in the face?

It was all right for Guv. Sure, his old man had cleared off, but at least Tony McGovern had the decency to leave Liverpool for a few years. He didn't just walk round the corner and move in with his worst enemy's mum! Even a non-person's better than one who hangs round to humiliate you every day of your life. What's more, Guv's mum had always been there for him. What about this? She had the gall to invite Maggot to stay. No warning, no nothing, just that stupid chess set to tell him he couldn't even shut out the nightmare in his own home. He shuddered at the thought of seeing Maggot at the breakfast table every morning, droning on about some stupid rubbish – *teacher* rubbish. Between them, Mum and Dad were going to make him a laughing stock.

It was about the time he bounced over the kerb on to Rice Lane that he started to wonder. 'Where am I going?'

Not home. Not to Mum and lover boy and *I love you really*. Sure, but not as much as Maggot.

Not to Carl Bain's. *Obviously* not there.

Not to South Parade. There are some things you can't talk about. Not even to your mates. So where? He

—— 115 ——

found himself on Rawcliffe Road, facing the entrance to the City Farm. Sure, why not? Talk to the animals.

'I bet I get more sense from a scabby old billy goat than from Mum and Dad,' he said out loud.

The rain had lessened, slowing to a fine, blowy drizzle. It didn't seem to make much difference. He certainly couldn't get any wetter. Padlocking his bike to a low picket fence he headed for the horses. They'd always been his favourite. Something about their quiet strength. 'And the way you always know what to expect,' John told the old grey pony as it nuzzled for food. 'You don't make promises, do you? You don't break them, either.'

The City Farm was deserted. The storm had seen to that. As the clouds cleared and the sun began to filter blearily through the subsiding shower, John felt as if he were the last person in the world. He found himself smiling. He'd remembered the stupid duel with Carl up at Lakeland.

Giving the pony a last pat on the nose, he walked back to his bike. 'Last man standing?' he murmured. 'This isn't what I meant.'

Seven

Kev recognized the warning signs early.

'Anybody know what's bugging O'Hara?' he hissed as John went to the toilet.

Shakes of the head all round.

'Not even you, Ratso?' asked Kev. 'You've usually got your ear to the ground.'

'Got me this time, Guv,' said Ratso. 'I know the

same as you; his dad clearing off and all that. Funny, he seemed to be hacking it, though.'

'Everything all right?' Kev asked as John returned to the changing-room.

'Uh huh.'

Which was all Kev managed to glean. At that moment Ronnie appeared at the door.

'Ready, lads?'

'Ready.'

Ratso started rummaging in his bag.

'Lost something?' asked Kev.

'Nah,' he replied. 'I'm changing the tape.'

'How come?'

'The state of John,' Ratso answered, finding his tape. 'We need something really upbeat.'

'Good idea,' said Kev.

He'd never really believed in the power of Ratso's music, but this particular Sunday morning he would have tried anything. Rabbit's feet, magic spells, lucky black cats, anything. It wasn't butterflies he was feeling at the start of a new season, it was giant, man-eating moths. In his heart of hearts he knew they had a mountain to climb. Longmoor were a class act with a long history of trophies. Given the Diamonds' troubled summer, it looked an uneven contest.

Ratso's choice of music was calculated to put a spring in the Diamonds' step; a golden oldie: *Simply the best.*

Gerry Darke, the new Longmoor captain, was standing in the centre circle ready to toss for kick-off. Hearing the anthem beating out from Ratso's ghetto-blaster, he shook his head. 'Wishful thinking, or what?' he asked. 'Don't tell me you've forgotten who won the Championship last season?'

'I haven't forgotten,' said Kev. 'But we're going to have that title off you, you know.' For a moment he almost believed his own bravado. 'Nothing so certain.'

'Over our dead bodies,' said Jonathan Wright, the Longmoor keeper.

'That can be arranged,' snarled Ant, only too ready to up the stakes.

'Yeah,' said Longmoor's Steve Kemp. 'Like to show me how?'

There was simmering resentment between the two sides, mainly due to the Diamonds' victory over Longmoor in the Challenge Cup final. It was only the firm intervention of the ref that kept the lid on.

'OK, OK,' he said. 'Cool it, lads. This is football, not World War Three.'

'What's the difference?' muttered Ant.

Kev smiled. He was showing just the sort of aggression they'd need to get through their first, testing fixture.

Longmoor won the toss. 'We'll kick off,' said Gerry Darke, on their behalf.

They were soon stroking the ball around with poise and accuracy. It didn't take Mystic Meg to forecast that the boys in the green and white hoops would again be a team to reckon with.

'What's the matter with John?' Kev asked Jamie. 'I've seen more activity from pondweed. Think I should drop back?'

'Give him a chance,' Jamie answered. 'He'll get into his stride.'

Only he didn't. Ten minutes into the match Longmoor were running the Diamonds ragged. They had 80 per cent of the possession and their midfield dominance was the key to their performance.

'For crying out loud,' groaned Kev, stranded ten yards inside the Longmoor half, waiting for some service. 'What's up with him?'

John had moved out to the right. It's not that he didn't tackle or chase the ball. He was busy enough. What was missing from his play was any sense of where Ratso and Dougie were. It was like he was playing blindfold. The midfield trio just weren't playing as a unit so it came as no surprise when Longmoor scored the opening goal. Mark Ridley slipped a great ball through to Pete Howells, overlapping on the right.

'Where's John?' screamed Kev. 'He should be marking the div.'

But John was stranded ten yards behind the play. Howells' low cross was almost met by the boot of the fair-haired boy unknown to Kev, but Gord got in a heroic block.

'Yes!'

But the cheers turned to groans as the clearance fell to another Longmoor newcomer who chipped over the scrum and into the net.

'Who was that?' asked Kev, stunned by the boy's composure.

'Bobby Sutton,' said Jamie. 'Nosmo's cousin.'

'Figures,' said Kev.

Seven minutes later Sutton was in again, seizing on a loose ball from Jimmy. He tried his luck from twenty yards, but Daz was able to beat it out. Once more the ball fell neatly for Longmoor and Gerry Darke slid it home from five yards.

'I've got to do something about this,' said Kev.

As he made a bee-line for his midfielders he saw John walking away.

'Where do you think you're going?' he rapped.

'Leave it,' said John. 'I'm not in the mood.'

'Not in the mood?' cried Kev. He looked around for support. 'Not in the pigging mood! What's that supposed to mean?'

John's shoulders sagged. 'Just leave me alone.'

For a few moments Kev was speechless.

'But John,' he said in the end. 'I'm relying on you. We all are.'

'Well don't,' said John. 'I'm not worth it.'

'Problems?' asked Jamie, jogging back.

'Not half,' said Kev. 'Looks like we've got to reorganize.'

But Longmoor came hunting before he could have any effect on the Diamonds' shambolic midfield. Gerry Darke beat Joey for pace out on the right, cut in and released Phil Gallacher. Longmoor had gone three-nil up.

'This is a nightmare,' said Kev. 'I'm going back in midfield. Right, lads,' he announced, clapping his hands, 'we've got ten minutes left of the half. Let's just reach the interval without conceding another.'

With Kev's tackling and some tremendous saves by Daz, the Diamonds did just that. They survived even if it was by the skin of their teeth.

'I think you know what I'm going to say, lads,' Ronnie began. 'You were very poor. There was no cohesion. I don't think you put together more than two consecutive passes. And the marking! Longmoor must think all their Christmasses have come at once. Kev's already done what I was going to suggest by dropping deep. John and Dougie ...'

They avoided his eyes.

'... You've got to get involved.'

Kev saw the expression on John's face.

'Fat chance,' he whispered to Jamie.

The arrival of Luke Costello almost put Kev off his half-time orange.

'How are you doing, McGovern?' he asked.

'Get lost.'

'Now that's not very nice,' said Costello.

He was accompanied by Brain Damage, Tez Cronin, Mattie and Carl. They were wearing their new red strip like a badge of honour. Things were obviously going their way.

'We're four-one up,' said Brain Damage. 'You?'

'If you must know,' Ratso told them, 'we're losing three-nil. That's right, you've got something to gloat about. Now take a hike.'

'Gladly,' said Costello. 'Three-nil, eh? You've just made my day.'

Carl was the last to return to the pitch where the Liver Bird were making such a convincing start to the season. He went over to John.

'I'm made up you're losing,' he said coldly. 'It's good to see you O'Haras suffer. It almost makes up for having to put up with your old man in my house.' A flash of hurt crossed his face, an expression John recognized all too well. 'Almost.'

It was an odd feeling. They had a common bond of suffering, but it didn't stop them being enemies. John had almost felt sympathy, but he was soon over his momentary weakness. Carl made sure of that.

'I don't know what's wrong with Mum,' said Carl. 'She can do better than him. He's a pig.'

John just remained seated on the ground, hugging his knees. Who's arguing? he thought.

'What's up, O'Hara?' asked Carl. 'Cat got your tongue? Bottling out again, I suppose. Just like on holiday.'

Ratso overheard the entire encounter.

'Don't tell me you're going to let him get away with that,' he said indignantly.

'Ratso,' said John, 'just forget it, eh?'

For the first five minutes of the second half, John faded just as ineffectively away from the action areas.

'Oh, come on, John,' said Kev, fighting down the desire to scream at him. 'Get stuck in.'

'Useless get,' stormed Ant. 'Longmoor are laughing at us. And that Liver Bird outfit.'

John looked across to Pitch Six where Liver Bird had just scored. Carl was striding round the centre circle, arms raised. Anger struck him in the guts like a fist.

'Arrogant beggar,' seethed John. 'Look at him. Think you've won, do you, Carl Bain?'

And that was it. No way was he going to win. No way would Carl be the last man standing.

'Bottled it, have I?' said John. 'We'll see about that. The duel isn't over yet.'

Seeing Mark Ridley getting away from Dougie, John raged after him. Curling a leg round Mark's he came away with the ball.

'Great tackle,' enthused Kev. 'Knock it over, John lad.'

John passed it and watched the Diamonds moving forwards. He glimpsed Ant looking at him.

'Got something to say, Ant?' he asked.

'No,' said Ant, scarcely able to believe the transformation. 'Nothing at all.'

Two minutes later John got in another vital tackle

and rolled the ball to Kev. He'd helped steady the ship and Kev was able to support Jamie up front. When Kev put Bashir away on the left, the little winger made the most of it. Getting behind the defence he whipped in a wicked cross. Barging between two defenders Jamie just got on the end of it.

Three-one.

'More like it, lads,' shouted Kev. 'Keep it coming.'

John's next tackle was less convincing. Bobby Sutton was moving at speed and his momentum almost carried him on. Almost. Dougie was covering and came away with the ball.

'Mine!' yelled Jamie.

Taking the pass in his stride he flicked it on to Kev, who cooly put it away.

Three-two.

With five minutes to go it was obvious that Longmoor had completely lost the script. Gord rose to meet a Jimmy Mintoe corner. Nodding it down into the crowded box, he found Bashir who flashed it into the net. Three-all,' yelled Jamie excitedly. 'We've done it.'

But there was still time on the clock. It turned out to be the two minutes that broke the Diamonds' hearts. Sensing that the Diamonds had dropped their guard, Steve Kemp launched a mighty kick downfield. Dougie Long who had been growing in confidence ran to meet it.

'Let it drop,' shouted John, his skin suddenly prickling with apprehension. 'Control it.'

But Dougie wasn't listening. Keen to get it back downfield for an improbable winner, he swung at it. Missing his kick completely, he left Bobby Sutton with only Daz to beat.

Four-three to Longmoor.

The moment the ref blew for full time a relieved Gerry Darke hurried over to confront Kev.

'Going to take the title off us, are you, McGovern? That's a laugh.'

The rest of the Diamonds were crushed by the defeat. Not Kev. 'Kid yourself if you want, Gerry,' he retorted, 'but we ran you off the park second half. We'll be there at the death, and you know it.'

Gerry walked away shaking his head.

'Didn't gloat for long, did he, Guv?' said Jamie, pleasantly surprised.

'That's because we rattled them,' said Kev. 'There's no disgrace in a defeat like that. We can learn from it.'

'Sorry, Guv,' said John, plucking up the courage to face his skipper. 'That was my fault.'

'Forget it,' said Kev, stunning his team-mates by his easy acceptance of defeat. 'I never thought we could win in the first place. We're going to get stronger, and Gerry knows it.'

'So you don't want to kill me?' asked John.

'Nah,' said Kev. 'That second-half performance, it was brilliant. You've never played that well before. Keep playing like that and we really could win the Championship.'

As Kev trotted over to talk to Ronnie, Jamie nudged John in the ribs. 'Think he's sickening for something?'

'Beats me,' said John.

He watched Kev talking animatedly to the manager. He knew by the glances in his direction that they were discussing his second-half recovery.

'I know one thing, though,' said John.

'What's that?'

'It's the last time I let the side down.' He thought of all the times he'd been let down. 'The last time ever!'

Eight

I meant it, what I said to John. Losing's never fun, but sometimes you learn more from losing something. I learned two things today. The first was pretty obvious; we were stretched too thin. We need a bigger squad and most of all we need a genuine out-and-out striker. OK, so I scored our second goal but my heart just isn't in playing up front. I was always looking back, wanting to get in a tackle, wanting to mix it with the opposition. My place is in the engine room. A steadying hand in midfield is worth a hat trick to a team.

The other thing I learned was about the character of the side. We were three-nil down and the game was spinning out of control. I mean, we were heading for a complete drubbing. Then, out of the blue, we dragged ourselves back into it and we almost snatched victory. We were lions in the second half, and nobody more so than John. I don't think I really believed he had it, the gift, but it's there, all right. Every tackle bit, every pass found a yellow shirt. He's just gone to hell and back with that family of his and he's proved he can take it. The pain is like a primed missile. The only question is who it's aimed at – you or some other poor moron. Well, I think John knows now. For so long, he's felt the pain in his guts and just taken the punishment. Now he's learning to use it, to stand up and fight back.

Maybe he could even teach me a thing or two. For weeks I've been turning myself inside out, wondering what to do:

You can trust John, he'll be good. Forget the dweeb, he'll be rubbish.

Stand up to Dad, that's your mate he's hurting. Back off, he's your dad, for goodness sake.

The team's OK, we won the Cup. The team's heading for disaster, we just don't have the squad.

Well, I've come to my senses at last. I'm off to see Uncle Dave. Watch this space.

Nine

John started at the voice behind him.

'Are you OK, John?' asked Sarah.

'For crying out loud, Sarah,' he cried. 'Haven't you ever heard of knocking?'

'Sorry,' said Sarah. 'What are you looking at?'

John gestured her over to his bedroom window. 'That lanky prat.'

His window overlooked the small garden where The Invader was.

'What's he doing?' asked Sarah as she peered at the tall figure of Maggot. He was tracing patterns in the air with his hands while performing a slow, ritual dance.

'Exercises,' snorted John. 'Tai Chi, or something. It's Japanese.'

'Chinese,' Sarah corrected. 'I think Simon had a go at it once.'

'Figures,' said John. 'That's just the sort of lamebrain thing Beano would do. Like tennis without a ball.'

Sarah pointedly ignored the jibe. 'He said it was very relaxing. Loads of Chinese people do it.'

'Well, let him go and do it in rotten China,' said

—— 126 ——

John. 'Better still, the North Pole. Yes, then he could freeze to death.' His voice broke a little. 'What did she have to let him stay for?'

'You tell me,' said Sarah. 'I don't know what Mum sees in him. Did you hear him playing that guitar? I think he was serenading her.'

They did a quick finger-down-the-throat. Then laughed.

John sucked his bottom lip. 'Music to throw up by. He's one of those hippies. You could take him to university with you.'

Sarah smiled. 'They don't have hippies in universities any more,' she said.

'So what do they have?'

'Geniuses – like me.'

There was a long pause as they watched Maggot continuing his exercises.

'John,' Sarah began tentatively.

'Uh huh.'

'You know what I told you. About getting a flat with Simon.'

'Mm.'

'Well, we've found a place. We're off next week.'

'Next week! I thought you said October.'

John's mind was racing. In just a few days he would be alone. Alone with *them*.

'You knew I was going,' said Sarah.

'Yes, but not this soon. I mean, what if he moves in? For good.'

Sarah's announcement felt like betrayal.

'I didn't make you any promises,' said Sarah.

John gave a wry smile. 'No, not like them.'

'I know it's tough,' she said. 'And I feel really tight running out on you. It's just ...'

—— 127 ——

John supplied the answer. 'You can't stand being here.'

'No,' Sarah agreed. 'I can't. Especially if that ...' She struggled for the right word, but gave up. 'If that *person* moves in. I've been putting up with Mum and Dad's stupid games for as long as I can remember. This is the last straw.'

'At least you've got somewhere to go,' said John. 'And somebody to be with. Not like me.'

'You've got somebody,' said Sarah. 'Quite a lot of somebodies, actually. Those Diamonds seem a good crowd.'

John could hardly believe his ears. Sarah saying something good about his footy team! They'd always been a shower of snotty oiks till then.

She must have read the expression on his face because she immediately added: 'I mean it. OK, so I don't see anything in this football nonsense, but they're your friends.'

'Yes,' said John, 'they are. I let them down last week.'

'Did you? How?'

'Oh, it was all this.' John waved his arms. 'Mum, Dad, Maggot, the whole mixed-up mess. I just let it all get to me.'

'Hardly surprising,' said Sarah. 'It would get to anybody. I feel like I've had this scream inside me all these years, just waiting to come out.'

John laughed.

'What's up?'

'You don't keep it all that hidden,' he told her. 'You always let them know what you think.'

'Do I?'

'Not half. I think they're even a bit scared of you.'

Sarah glanced down at Maggot. 'He's coming in,' she said.

'I'll miss you,' said John.

'That's the second time you've told me that,' said Sarah. 'My soppy little brother.'

'So? It's true. Who's going to protect me from Mum and Dad.'

Sarah gave him a level stare. 'Something tells me you're toughening up,' she said. 'Not long ago you seemed to spend all your time moping around expecting the sky to fall in. You've changed lately. You seem … stronger.'

'You reckon?'

'Yes, I do.'

'Wow,' said John. 'Stronger, eh?'

He held up his arm and flexed his bicep. At least, that's what he tried to do. Only nothing showed.

'I meant,' Sarah said, 'strong here.' She tapped his forehead.

'It's all right,' said John. 'I know exactly what you mean. Tell you what.'

'What?'

'Come and watch us on Sunday.'

'*Me*, at a football match?'

'Yes. Bring Beano, if you want. It's special, Sarah. A grudge match.'

'Why, what's so important about it?'

'For starters, Carl Bain's on the other side.'

'Oh.'

'Oh is right. And you know that gang who are always after us?'

Sarah nodded. 'Andy Ramage's crew. Oh, I know all about them. They robbed the wheel off Simon's bike.'

'They never.'

'They did. Then they hung it from the top of that big tree by the Community Centre.'

John laughed. 'Sorry, I can just imagine Beano's face.'

Sarah tried to be serious but a moment later she joined in the laughter.

'So you'll come?' asked John.

'Yes,' said Sarah. 'I'll come.'

Just then Mum popped her head round the door. 'You two sound happy,' she said.

Sarah was as sharp as ever. 'Oh, I wouldn't go that far.' Then she winked at John. 'Not yet, anyway.'

Ten

The changing-room was unusually quiet that Sunday morning. Tension hung around the Diamonds like a mist.

'I suppose you all know that they're both playing,' said Ant, finally breaking the silence. 'Dirty rotten turncoats.'

Everybody knew who he meant, especially John. It had been on his mind for days. He'd be contesting the midfield with his old enemy. And Carl would be partnered by his partner in crime, Mattie.

'Just don't let yourself get drawn into any rough stuff,' said Kev. 'Remember the game against Blessed Hearts at the end of last season. We all know Costello's game plan. Tackle to maim, foul to kill. Even if you don't get your man, you'll probably sting him into getting cautioned.'

There was an audible intake of breath. The Guv'nor

advising non-retaliation – it was like a tiger turning vegetarian!

'What are you all looking at?' he demanded.

'Nothing, Guv,' said Jimmy. 'Just wondering when you were getting your halo, that's all.'

'OK,' said Kev, 'so I've risen to it myself once or twice, but we've got to stay disciplined today. Our squad is too thinly stretched to react to their aggro.'

Ratso wasn't taking part in the conversation. Instead he was scribbling furiously on a piece of paper.

'What's with the writing?' asked Jamie. 'Lost interest in the game or something?'

'Oh, I'm interested, all right,' said Ratso. 'I've just come up with another reason we've got to hammer these morons into the ground.'

Daz looked interested. Hammer them. Ratso was talking his language. 'Which is?'

Ratso waved his scrap of paper. 'I've just worked it out. The Liver Bird are top of the table on goal difference, ahead of Ajax, Longmoor and Northend.'

'Behave, Ratso,' said Joey. 'We've only played one game. It doesn't mean a thing.'

'So?' said Ratso. 'The Liver Bird are still top and that means we've got to knock them off their perch.'

'Ha hardy ha,' said Daz. 'Your jokes don't improve.'

There was a knock on the door. It was Ronnie. 'Right, lads, let's show these bozos what we're made of.'

Ant shook his head. 'Sounds more like Guv every day. Kevin McGovern,' he chuckled, 'you're a terrible influence on the older generation.'

Kev smiled.

'A few words in the shell-like,' said Ronnie. 'No getting drawn into ...'

'... Any rough stuff,' chorused the team.

Ronnie looked non-plussed.

'Guv's already done your team talk for you, Uncle Ron,' explained Jimmy.

'Oh,' said Ronnie. 'I see.'

As the boys filed out, Kev hung back to catch Bashir.

'Bash,' he whispered. 'Everything ready?'

Bashir nodded. 'Dad and your Uncle Dave are still down there. They were at it half the night.'

'Sound as a pound,' said Kev. 'I just can't wait to see the look on Lee Ramage's face.' Not to mention Dad's, he thought apprehensively.

'Come on, you two,' called Ronnie. 'Anybody would think you weren't looking forward to this morning.'

Kev winked at Bashir. Ronnie couldn't be further than the truth.

Kev almost had to peel Ant off Costello.

'Dirty fouling get!' bawled Ant.

Kev at last managed to wedge himself between them. It wasn't easy.

'Get a grip, Ant,' Kev panted. 'This is exactly what he wants.'

Ant pointed to the marks on his shin where Costello's studs had raked his leg. 'Yes, and he'll get it if he comes near me again.'

'Promises promises,' sneered Costello.

'Shove off,' warned Kev, 'or I'll let him at you.'

'Aw, what's up?' said Brain Damage, his voice dripping with sarcasm. 'Losing, are you?'

Kev's neck prickled with humiliation. It had been the nightmare start. Costello had launched the ball hopefully downfield right from the kick-off, catching Daz unawares. Backpedalling desperately, Daz had managed to tip the ball over the bar for a corner. Unfortunately, the Diamonds were no more alert as the ball dropped into the danger area. In a vicious goalmouth scramble Daz was flattened by an elbow. While the Diamonds' defenders appealed unsuccessfully for a foul, Carl Bain of all people was there to poke the ball home from close range.

One-nil down.

'Poor, poor Diamonds,' added Brain Damage.

'I'm having him as well,' raged Ant.

'Knock it off, will you?' Kev pleaded. 'There's plenty of time to equalize.'

Ant was quivering with anger. 'It was Brain Damage that fouled Daz in the first place,' he seethed. 'He elbowed him in the face. I saw him do it.'

'I know, I know,' said Kev, 'but the ref didn't, so it stands. Now let's get back on terms.'

John was storming down the touch line. Carl pigging Bain! Why did it have to be him? Dad's appearance five minutes earlier, in the company of Carl's mum, hadn't helped his spirits.

'Hey, O'Hara,' shouted Carl. 'Still think you can win our duel? Or have you bottled out again?'

'It's still on,' said John irritably. 'Last man standing.'

'That's exactly what I wanted to hear,' said Carl.

In the next ten minutes the play was condensed into the centre of the park. Tackles were flying in and neither side could put together more than two passes. It was fast and furious and no place for the squeamish. Nobody was under more pressure than Kev as Brain Damage and Costello doubled up to muscle him out of it.

'Come on, John,' he appealed, after being propelled

across the centre circle by a particularly brutal challenge. 'Give me some support.'

'Sorry, Guv,' said John. He realized he'd drifted out of the game. He just couldn't take his eyes off Dad and Carl's mum. Parents! Boy, don't some kids have them. Maggot at home, her at the game. They'd got him in a pincer movement.

Bashir finally broke through for the Diamonds just before half-time, gleefully seizing on Ratso's headed clearance of a Liver Bird attack.

'Run it, Bash!' yelled Kev, just before he was viciously sandwiched by Brain Damage and Costello.

Bashir didn't need any encouragement. Sprinting down the left flank he glanced up for an outlet. Hovering in space was Jamie, the Diamonds' lone striker who'd been keeping a dogged vigil up front for most of the half.

'My ball,' he shouted, making a diagonal run into the box. Shaking himself free of his marker, Jamie met the ball with a sweet, glancing header that beat Tony Cross in the Liver Bird goal all ends up.

One-all.

'Hey, Bain,' said John, 'ready for a pasting?' Then, with feeling, 'Like I started to give you on holiday.'

John glimpsed Dad's disapproving frown.

'A bit uncalled for,' he said, as much for the benefit of Carl's mum as for John.

'You reckon?' said John. 'Well, tough, Dad because the snidey little get's going to get what he deserves.'

Without another word John raced off to rejoin the action. What right did his old man have to look down on anybody? Instead, he searched for Sarah. She was jumping up and down, giving him the thumbs-up. Even Beano was starting to enjoy the match.

'No going to sleep now, lads,' warned Kev. 'Keep your minds on the job in hand.'

John took it as a personal instruction. In the ten minutes up to the interval he was part of every move the Diamonds made, intercepting passes, tracking back, sliding in with the vital tackle.

'That's it, John,' said Kev. 'I knew you could do it.'

With Costello and Brain Damage shadowing Kev's every move, John had the freedom to dictate the pace of play. The tide was turning the Diamonds' way.

John scanned the spectators, taking in Dad and his divvy girlfriend and Carl with his stupid, twisted glare.

Kev noticed his set jaw and steely glare. 'I tell you what, John lad, you really look like you mean it this morning.'

'Mean it?' John repeated. 'Guv, you have no idea.'

Eleven

'What was all that about?' demanded Dad as he drew John aside during half-time. 'You didn't half show me up talking to me like that.'

John threw his arms up with exasperation. '*I* showed *you* up! What planet are you from, Dad?'

Dad's voice descended to a low growl. 'Meaning?'

'Oh, forget it.'

'Come back here,' shouted Dad, reaching for John's arm.

John stamped over to where his team-mates were taking their orange.

'Trouble?' asked Kev.

'Nothing I can't handle,' John replied.

'Sure?'

John smiled. He'd read somewhere about an elephant that carried the weight of the world on his shoulders. He was starting to realize you didn't even have to be an elephant to have a burden to shoulder.

'Positive. I just want to win.'

'You know what you've got to do, then,' said Kev, about to launch into one of his lectures.

'Of course I do,' said John. '*Stay focussed. Know what you want and think of nothing else.*'

'Do I say it that often?' asked Kev.

'Guv,' said Jamie, chipping in, 'you say nothing else.'

Bashir leaned over. 'We're ready to re-start.'

'OK, lads,' said Kev. 'Let's take the game to them.'

Crossing the pitch the Diamonds were all high fives and gritted teeth.

'Up for it, aren't they?' said Beano.

'All of a sudden,' Sarah replied, 'our John's up for anything.'

It was fifteen minutes into the second half before Costello started to realize that doubling up on Kev was giving the Diamonds other options. Far from snuffing out the main threat, their concentration on Kev was allowing John and Ratso to put their passing game together. Jamie was starting to get some service and the Liver Bird attack was a spent force.

'Andy,' Costello told Brain Damage, 'leave McGovern to me. You and Carl get into O'Hara.'

The first John knew of the change of tactics by the Liver Bird was a shooting pain in his ankle. Carl and Brain Damage had come in from behind with their studs showing.

'You animals!' roared Ant, piling in. 'You could have broken his leg.'

—— 136 ——

It was a disgusting tackle on the leg he'd hurt on holiday. Carl had gone for it on purpose.

John met his eyes for a moment, then cast aside thoughts of retaliation. He knew what Kev expected of him. Ignoring the pain in his ankle, he hauled himself to his feet and blocked Ant's advance.

'Leave it, Ant,' he said. 'I'm fine.'

'But they shouldn't be allowed to get away with it,' complained Ant.

'It was me they fouled,' John insisted. 'I'll handle it, thank you very much. Just keep your cool.'

And that's exactly what the Diamonds did. Riding the tackles, hurdling the challenges, they played their own game constructing triangles of passes and patiently building their attacks. They had the Liver Bird chasing round getting ever more frustrated.

'This is it,' said Kev approvingly. 'Ole football.'

Then just when he started to wonder if it wasn't all getting a little too intricate, John dispossessed Carl, breaking up a rare Liver Bird attack.

'Boot it forward!' yelled Kev. 'Look for Jamie.'

But John had other options. Jimmy was racing down the left with Bashir outside him. Switching the play, John found Jimmy who flicked it on to Bashir. The winger's first time cross found Jamie.

Two-one.

'You're finished,' John told Carl.

'And you're dead,' said Carl.

A moment later John saw him in a huddle with Mattie and Brain Damage. It worried him for a moment, but there was a match to win. With minutes to go, a tiring Dougie Long gave the Liver Bird their first scoring chance of the half. Costello intercepted his feeble pass and put Carl clear. Jimmy was after Carl as well, but John knew it was down to him. Sprinting across, he closed on Carl.

'He's mine,' he told Jimmy. 'You cover the area.'

On a surface that was still hard from the summer sunshine, Carl was struggling to control the ball. John saw his chance. Carl was already in the penalty area. The tackle had to be a good one. Curling his leg round Carl's he got a clean touch on the ball. As it ran free Jimmy was available to make the clearance.

'Flipping brilliant, John!' enthused Daz. 'I could kiss you.'

'No,' said John firmly. 'No you couldn't.'

To make absolutely sure, John raced downfield to join the developing Diamonds' attack. He was aware of Mattie, Carl and Brain Damage hot on his heels. They were out to do him some mischief. He knew that if he had any sense he would pull out now and get out of danger's way. But he didn't have that sort of sense – he had the will to win.

'My ball,' he cried, finding himself clear and only twenty yards from the Liver Bird goal.

Ratso was in possession. Spotting the loose man he threaded the ball between Jelly Wobble and Tez Cronin. As John prepared to pull the trigger the chasing pack crashed into him. He tumbled under the scrum of players. First a fist, then a boot smashed into him.

'Get off him!' came a voice like a thunderbolt.

A moment later John rolled on to his back, his face creased with the pain in his side and shoulder.

'I feel like I've been run over,' he said.

'So what?' said Kev. 'You've only won us a penalty.'

John picked himself up and looked around. Jamie was placing the ball on the spot. Brain Damage was sitting on the ground, nursing his cheek. John knew from the sly grin on Ant's face that he'd got on the ref's blind side and finally settled the score from the first minute foul on Daz.

'Mattie and Carl?'

Kev grinned. 'They've got their marching orders.'

John saw them trooping off the pitch, heads bowed.

Jamie took two steps then jogged forward and stroked the ball just inside the left upright.

'Three-one,' said Kev loudly, directing his comments at Costello and the fallen Brain Damage. 'With a two-goal cushion and two of your players off the field, I think we've got it sewn up.'

John was equally jubilant. 'Hey, Bain,' he shouted at Carl's back. 'Remember the duel? Looks like I win.'

He saw Dad glaring at him. He seemed more bothered about John offending Carl's mum than about him getting kicked to a pulp. John remembered the elephant. The world didn't seem all that heavy.

'Not so cocky now, are you, Carl? Who's the last man standing?'

Twelve

It didn't come as much of a surprise when there was a reception committee waiting for the victorious Diamonds.

'Hey Gooly, what do you think of our Lee's new premises?' Brain Damage wasn't about to give them any breathing space. He started right in. 'Pity about what happened to yours.'

Bashir ignored him. Instead he eyed the red and

white frontage and the sign: *Ramage Taxi Hire*. Lee Ramage and Tony McGovern were talking to a couple of their drivers.

'It's not right, is it, Bash?' said Jamie. 'Your dad's place gets trashed and those low-lifes open up next door. I bet I know what sort of thing those taxis will be carrying.'

Then he remembered Kev standing next to him. 'Guv, I'm sorry. I never meant ...'

'Forget it, Jay,' said Kev. 'I'm not proud of what my dad does.'

The gang were keeping up a barrage of abuse, but the Diamonds ignored them. It sounded too much like sour grapes.

'You must be gutted, Bash,' said Ant.

'Not really,' said Bashir cheerfully.

Ant and Jamie exchanged glances. The other Diamonds looked equally bewildered.

'But they're the ones that wrecked the shop,' said Jimmy, 'and they're rubbing your nose in it.'

'That's right,' said Gord. 'They're laughing at you.'

'Let them,' said Bashir coolly. 'We'll have the last laugh, won't we, Guv?'

Kev smiled. 'That's right, Bash.' He glanced at his watch. 'I wonder what's keeping Uncle Dave.' He was looking up South Parade.

'What's going on?' asked Joey. 'Is there something you haven't told us?'

'I hope there is,' said Kev, consulting his watch again. 'They're late. You don't think something's wrong, do you, Bash?'

Bashir frowned. 'I don't know.'

Kev found himself stealing glances at his dad and Lee Ramage. Had they rumbled his plan? Is that why

Uncle Dave and Bashir's dad hadn't arrived? His answer came with a mechanical whirring. The security shutters on the Mini Mart had started to open.

'What's going on?' asked Ratso, turning round.

The rising shutters had attracted the attention of Ramage and Kev's dad. Costello and Brain Damage pressed forward.

'This some sort of trick?' asked Brain Damage.

'No trick,' said Kev proudly. 'Just the grand opening of the shop.'

As the shutter finally reached the top of the shop front the Diamonds burst into spontaneous applause. In the doorway of the refurbished Mini Mart stood Kev's Uncle Dave and Mr Gulaid.

'What are you playing at?' demanded Lee Ramage angrily. 'I thought ...'

'Go on,' said Uncle Dave, 'what exactly did you think? That you'd put Mr Gulaid out of business? Is that what you thought too, Tony?'

Kev's dad shifted his feet nervously. 'You be careful what you're saying. Neither of us had anything to do with the damage to the shop.'

'No,' said Mr Gulaid, 'of course not. It's a coincidence that you were threatening my business just before it happened.'

Their raised voices didn't go unnoticed. The newsagent from further up the Parade was watching from his shop doorway.

'Watch your mouth,' snarled Ramage. 'Or I'll —'

'Or you'll what?' asked Ronnie, arriving at the scene. He'd decided to catch up with his team. He suspected trouble after the match. 'There are witnesses, remember.'

'Go on,' said Uncle Dave. 'Tell us what you're going

to do.' He held up a pocket tape recorder. 'The police might find it interesting listening.'

'I'll tell you what we're going to do,' said Kev's dad, snatching the tape recorder. 'We're taking this for a start.'

Lee Ramage shoved his face into Mr Gulaid's. 'I'm having you off this Parade,' he spat. 'No way are you staying next door to me. I'm not having anybody poking their nose into my business.'

'I'm going nowhere,' said Mr Gulaid.

'No?' said Ramage, shoving Mr Gulaid back. 'Well, we'll see about that.'

Kev watched is dismay as Dad stepped in front of Ronnie and Uncle Dave.

'I think we should allow them to sort this by themselves,' he said.

Kev couldn't stand it any longer and threw himself at Dad. 'Stop it!' he cried. 'Stop it or I'll hate you forever.'

Dad looked startled, but not as startled as when a police car pulled up in front of him.

'We've received a call,' said the officer. 'One of the shopkeepers said there was an affray on the Parade.'

Kev glanced towards the newsagent. A smile.

'Oh, there's no problem here,' said Uncle Dave. 'Is there, Tony?'

Kev watched Dad backing off slowly. Behind him, Ramage glared first at the shop then at Mr Gulaid and Uncle Dave before making for his car. 'You haven't heard the last of this,' he shouted. 'Come on, Tony. Let's get out of here.'

As Ramage drummed his fingers on the dashboard in a fit of rage, Kev's dad followed. He paused by Kev.

'This was down to you somehow, wasn't it?' he asked, indicating the refurbished shop.

Kev nodded. Crazy as it might seem, he couldn't look dad in the eye.

'Did you have something to do with the phone call too, son?'

Kev's heart was racing. He wished he had. But he'd done more than enough. He knew he'd done the right thing.

'Uh-huh.'

'Well, thanks a lot, son. You've made me look a right idiot.'

Kev averted his eyes. He hated himself for it, but he felt almost as guilty doing the right thing as he had when Dad wrecked the shop.

'You're wrong, Tony,' said Uncle Dave. 'You did that by yourself. Only an idiot would get involved with that character.' He indicated Ramage. 'You're a loser, man. But your boy doesn't have to be.'

Uncle Dave rested a hand protectively on Kev's shoulder. Kev was glad of the reassurance.

Dad gave him one last look, then slid into the driver's seat of Ramage's BMW and roared away. After a couple of minutes the police car followed suit.

'That was priceless,' said Uncle Dave. 'I'd have paid to see them get their come-uppance.'

Kev noticed Costello and Co sidling away. It was their second defeat that day.

'How did you do it though, Kev?' asked John.

'I had this idea,' said Kev. 'Uncle Dave used to work making furniture units. So I thought, why not suggest he does a bit on the shop.'

'A bit?' laughed Uncle Dave. 'Me and Hassan were locked in there for the best part of a week.'

Mr Gulaid smiled.

'We did it though, didn't we, David?'

'Not half.'

Kev had detached himself from the crowd outside the Mini Mart.

'I bet you're chuffed,' said John, joining him. 'You really put one over on the Ramages. Two, if you count the game as well.'

'Yes,' said Kev. There was a hint of uncertainty in his voice.

'Hey, don't go soft on me,' said John, recognizing the tone. 'Remember what you always tell me. Stay focussed on the main thing. Blot everything else out of your mind.'

Kev stared up the road were Dad had just driven. 'Even when it's my dad?'

John nodded. 'I've come to a conclusion about parents,' he said. 'They're a bit like buses. Great when they're working properly, but you can always walk instead. You can do without if you have to.'

Kev smiled thinly. 'And you really believe that?'

It was John's turn to give a humourless smile. 'I'm trying to. Hard, isn't it?'

Kev nodded. 'Yes, dead hard. I think I did the right thing back there. You know, over the shop.'

'You did,' John assured him.

'So how come I still feel so rotten?'

John shrugged his shoulders. 'If I knew the answer to that,' he said, 'I wouldn't be spending half my life wishing I was somebody else.'

'That bad, eh?'

'Yes.'

'Still,' said Kev, 'we got a result today, didn't we?'

'Dead right,' John answered. 'And that's all that matters.'

With another glance up the road Kev nodded: 'Sure, that's all that matters.'

Thirteen

That Liver Bird game was a crossroads. There was so much at stake. Lose, and it could have taken weeks to rebuild our morale. Let's face it, Costello and Co would have haunted us everywhere we went. We'd never have lived it down. But we've stopped the rot after that opening day defeat, and a lot of the credit goes to John. I used to think he was a real divvy. He never stopped moaning, but he isn't the pathetic wimp I always took for him. It took real steel to handle his mum and dad's performance. I've got a lot of time for somebody, who can crawl over broken glass and come up fighting. He was there when we needed him most. Now we can go forward. Next week those brothers come back off holiday, so they can show us what they're made of.

I haven't seen Dad since Sunday. He was supposed to take me and Gareth out tonight, but he never showed. Some things never change. Great, isn't it? I stood by my mate and did what was right and I still end up feeling rotten. John's probably sitting at home right now thinking the same thing. But at least we did what was right and that counts for something.

Doesn't it?

Other books you will enjoy in the TOTAL FOOT-BALL series

Some You Win ...

'There's me with my mind full of the beautiful game ... and what are we really – a bunch of deadbeats ...'

But Kev has a reputation to live up to and when he takes over as captain of the Rough Diamonds he pulls the team up from the bottom of the league, and makes them play to win ... every match.

Under Pressure

'The pressure's on. Like when you go for a fifty-fifty ball. Somebody's going to blink, and it isn't me. Ever.'

Kev, captain of the Rough Diamonds, acts swiftly when too many of the lads just aren't playing the game and let pressures off the pitch threaten the team's future.

Divided We Fall

'If you don't take risks you're nothing. There's only half an inch of space between determination and dirty play and I live in it.'

That's the law Kev McGovern lays down for the Rough Diamonds on the pitch, but what about off it? When Kev's best mate Jamie's world is wrecked by dirty play he's desperate to get everything back to safe, reliable normal.

'Some people have all the luck. Dave Lafferty for one. How else do you explain a kid who's brilliant at everything? I would have given my right arm to swop with Dave.'

But Kev is stunned when he discovers that Dave has to cope with epilepsy. When he suffers a major attack, the victory the Rough Diamonds are so desperate to win, the longed-for junior league challenge cup, hangs precariously in the balance.